MALICIOUS

DESIRES

MALICIOUS

DESIRES

WRONGFUL DESIRES #1

By Caz May

First Published 2024
Paperback ISBN 978-0-6454683-1-1
Published by Caz May
© Caz May 2023-2024
Cover editing by Caz May
Editing:by Samantha Wolf (Lunar Eclipse Designs)

For all those who believe in happy endings and thought that Romeo & Juliet shouldn't have had to die.

My only love sprung from my only hate, Too early seen unknown, and known too late! Prodigious birth of love is it to me, that I must love a loathed enemy.

William Shakespeare

AUTHOR'S PREFACE

This is a dark MM romance.
It features explicit language, explicit frequent sexual scenes which include snowballing, rimming, nipple play, sexsomnia, somnophilia, cum play, dub con, non con, expeditionism (public sex acts), on page torture and murder, Blood play, Knife play, Gun play, drug and alcohol use (and misuse) and other graphic on page violence. There is also mention of religious themes, and related bigotry.
Please read with caution if these are triggers for you. And reach out if you have any questions about the contents of this book before reading.
Please note this book is written in British/Australian English so some spelling and grammar may be different.
It is set in a fictional European city.
Caz May xx

For full content warnings please visit my website www.cazmayauthor.com

PLAYLIST

SCAN ME

Full playlist on Spotify

ALSO BY CAZ MAY

Secret Santa (A Christmas Rom-Com)
Jingle Balls

Lockgrove Bay Series

(Reading order as listed)

Be Tempted Duet

Bk 1-Loathing Temptation

Bk 2 Wicked Temptation

Bay Hearts Trilogy

Bk 1 Wild Hearts

Bk 2 Tamed Hearts

Bk 3 Unbreakable

(best read after Take my Heart)

My Heart Duet

Bk 1-Take My Heart

Dreams Duet

Bk 1 In Your Dreams

Bk 2 In My Dreams

My Girl Duet

Bk 1-Not my Girl
Bk 2-Still my Girl

Always Only You Series

Bk 1-Roommates Don't Kiss & Tell
Bk 2-Friends Don't Say Goodbye
Bk 3-Feelings Don't Play Fair
Bk 4-Hearts Don't Steer Us Wrong

The Mackenney Family Saga

Bk 1-Country Secrets
Bk 2-Doctor Attraction
Bk 3-Unlawful Attachment

Heart Voyager Duet

Bk 1-Let Time Be

X

In beautiful Vemore our story begins, where a family feud spanning generations is about to shatter when two young men, forbidden to associate fall in love.

CHAPTER ONE

REECE

Reckless should be my middle name. Reece 'Reckless' Montserrat. It's not but it should be—because I'm on the wrong side of the city—across the tracks in Capullo territory. If anyone sees me—or recognises my black Bugatti—I'll be done for. Most likely gunned down in cold blood by a Capullo nemesis. But still, I'm here, pulling into the petrol station. It's not my fault it's the only one closest to the best beach in Vemore that sells premium fuel. It's open twenty-four hours and usually, I visit to fuel up in the black of night, to blend in. But today, I'm being reckless. The Bugatti is so low on fuel that it's spluttering as I drive into the station. I cut the engine, knowing it won't start again without fuel.

I press the button and the doors lift so I can get out. I slide out of the seat and open the petrol cap.

CAZ MAY

Slipping the nozzle in, I fuel the car, absentmindedly glancing around so I'm not paying attention when it clicks off and I press it harder, causing fuel to spill out everywhere. It splashes down the side of my car, over my black combat boots and the concrete.

It's then that another car—a shitbox Mercedes convertible—pulls up behind me. I put the nozzle back in place in the bowser and the idiots jump out of their car without even opening the doors.

Such showoff wankers. They eye me, scoffing loudly.

"Well, look who it is, across the tracks scum," Blyth taunts, standing behind his master like a lost puppy dog. I prefer kitty cats, of the actual animal kind, not the pussy kind of a girl. I'd rather lick an actual cat's back and get a mouth full of fur than kiss a girl.

I take the nozzle again and hold it towards Tidus Capullo. His minions rise up like snakes to protect him, as though I'm honestly going to douse him in petrol when he's got a cigarette hanging between his lips. I'm not an idiot.

"Tidus," I mock, stepping towards him and poking his chest with the nozzle.

He hisses, "Reece." And we stare at each other, a showdown of sorts to show off.

"You planning on setting me alight?"

"I would never. But watching you go up in flames would be a sight."

"Likewise, scum, and I should burn thee for crossing into our territory and parading your wealth around as though you're welcome here."

Sneering, I replace the nozzle, taking a step backward to slide into the seat of my car. "Like I'd want to be in the vermin-infested side of Vemore, with the likes of you."

Tidus chuckles, clutching his stomach, and takes his cigarette out of his mouth to exhale the smoke in my face. It causes me to hack out a cough.

"The only vermin here is you, Reece," Tidus taunts, flicking his half spent cigarette across the petrol station as he jumps back into his Mercedes, with his dipshits following.

The flames start licking the fuel on the ground, and I floor it to drive away, my door barely closed as I spin the wheels, creating a flume of smoke from my tyres as I speed off. The stupid fuckers are crawling out of the fuel station, dangerously close to being engulfed by the increasing flames. I knew Tidus was a dimwit, but setting a fuel station alight, and staying to watch the carnage is fucking stupid. But I know it's a warning. They're watching me, tracking my every move and next time I won't be so lucky to drive away.

CAZ MAY

Driving off I meander around the streets of Vemore, listening to the scream of the sirens as they head to the carnage that Tidus has caused. He really is an idiot, and his minions are no better following him around as though he's a god. The whole Capullo family is like that, fucking do-gooders who think the whole damn city revolves around them and their pretentious arses.

I don't know Jasper Capullo well enough to comment on him, but Tidus has mentioned his cousin a time or two and he seems like a loser. One of those prissy boys—not in a hot sexy way—but in a babyish way. He's a recluse honestly, because he's my age and he's never been around the social scene much at all, even during high school when we were all forced to go to the only high school in Vemore. Montserrat vs Capullo was rife even then, and Jasper just preferred to spend his days hiding out in the library or art room so I'd heard.

For all know now, he's probably hot as fuck all grown up and not langly like he was when we were kids. I'd teased the shit out of him in primary school because he was all legs, and shy as shit—always hiding behind his blonde locks in his face—and I'd had a little crush on him. Crushing on Jasper Capullo—when I was ten—was when I first realised that I might be gay. It seemed normal to me to like guys—not girls—because voicing that to Malyk—my best mate—he outright blurted out that he likes dudes and I didn't think anything of it.

Telling my parents had been a ride though. Mum didn't talk to me for a month, and Dad just scoffed and then happily said, 'Well at least I won't have to pay for a lavish wedding.'

They were pissed off though, as it meant they couldn't force me to marry some rich girl of their choosing to uphold the Montserrat name and legacy. Don't get me wrong, I love being rich but purely only for the materialistic purpose, like the fact I didn't have to bat an eyelid at paying two million for my Bugatti. I hate that to have unlimited access to my 'trust fund' I have to do Dad's bidding, offing lowlife fuckers that owe him or have done him wrong. But a son's gotta do what he's gotta do to keep daddy happy, even more so when that son—me—is gay. If I want to be myself, that's what I have to endure.

Having driven around for the good part of an hour—eating into the fuel I just pumped— I pull up at Vemore Beach and get out of the Bugatti with my journal and pencil in hand from the seat beside me. I'm never without them. Writing in my journal—songbook—clears the chaos in my head, and helps me fight the demons and the images I'm forced to face from the killings I do. It's messed with my head a time or two and if I don't get it out on paper in lyrical form what I see in reality crashes into my nightmares and I wake up drenched in sweat screaming as though I'm the one being murdered.

Sitting under the cliffs, I open my journal, scribbling out random words to clear the clutter in my head.

Monster Beautiful Violent Vulgar Death Life Love

I want love in my life like anyone else, but I can't see anyone looking past my depravity, past the acts of violence I commit on a daily basis. I know I should be in a jail cell–for the rest of my life–without a key in sight for the number of murders I've committed, but the cops turn a blind eye to any violence or crime of any kind committed by a prestigious family of Vemore, be that a Montserrat or a Capullo.

My parents' limo drives up, the window rolling down so my father can glare at me. I ignore them, not giving a shit about what insult my father is hurling at me, or what he's requesting of me again. Instead, I flip them off and meander back to the Bugatti. I wait until they drive away before I get in and speed off in search of Malyk. He'd mentioned something about a night of debauchery coming up and I'm wondering–and hoping–it's tonight.

CHAPTER TWO

Jasper

Watching the news these days is like watching the world implode before your eyes, every single day. Vemore is going to hell, and I hate seeing it but can't stop myself from watching the news every night. It's just a ritual now. Something I do every day despite hating it. It's torture like going to the gym, which is my other ritual that I do every day right after I watch the news at 7 pm.

Tonight's news isn't really anything new, something else in our screwed up city going up in flames. But what strikes me is amidst the footage of the petrol station bursting into flames is my cousin's car driving away.

Tidus is a badass but stupid, clearly.

I pick up my phone and dial him.

"Cuz…" he greets me.

I don't reply with the same tone, blurting out, "Did you do it, Tidus?"

He chuckles in that annoying way that grates on my nerves.

"Do what, cuz?"

"Set the Mobil alight?"

"Can't say, cuz. Ears are listening."

I scoff, annoyed at him because it's certain he did something, had something to do with it and as usual he's hiding something.

"That tells me everything, Tidus."

"Not everything dear cousin."

"What are you trying to hide?"

"Our enemy was there. Trying to steal from us, even though he's richer than us."

I wrack my brain, trying to piece together what enemy he's referring to. Our only enemies in Vemore are the Montserrat's and most of the time they don't venture onto our side of the city.

"A Montserrat?" I question, my mind wondering if he's talking about my high school nemesis, the Reece Montserrat. The stares he'd give me—like he was stripping me naked in the corridors—sent me retreating to the library where I could hide away from him. Reece's stare made me feel odd, icky even.

"Yes, a Montserrat. Reece."

I gasp, "Oh."

Tidus laughs. "You still crushing on him?"

"I never was. I've only got eyes for Rebekah."

MALICIOUS DESIRES

"Well do something about it, dear cousin. She just broke up with her boyfriend."

"Um, yep…maybe at the frat ball," I stammer, my shyness showing through in my tone and words.

"When are you moving into the dorms?"

"Next week," I tell my cousin.

He chuckles again, inhaling as though he's taking a drag of a cigarette.

"You'll forget all about the sweet Rebekah when surrounded by girls in the dorm."

"Not a chance, Tidus," I respond without conviction. I haven't told Tidus, but I'm honestly no longer interested in Rebekah. I just want to get on with uni and forget about relationships of any kind. Tidus has always pushed me to explore sexually, but I haven't done anything except kiss a girl who was hiding out in the library one day. I didn't even know her name and kissing her wasn't that thrilling, so I haven't sought out to kiss anyone else or explore sex since.

"I beg to differ, cuz. Gotta go."

He hangs up without another word, and I flick the news off, sighing and standing from the bed. I haul my gym bag back onto the bed and continue to pack in my belongings that I want to take from my room to the dorms. A tear falls down my cheek when I pick up the photo of Grandpa Capullo. I

CAZ MAY

miss him so much. And I hate the Montserrat's for taking him away from us.

Thankfully Montserrat's are not welcome at Valley View University. It's Capullo territory and one of the only buildings still standing from before the feud between our families began. But if Reece is impeding on our side of the city, I'm sure something dangerous is afoot. And I'm a little worried–scared–about that prospect. But I'm equally intrigued to see Reece again. He was the epitome of a bad boy, and had started covering his body in tattoo's when we were only sixteen. The thought of tattoos has always intrigued me, art on the skin, but I haven't marred my skin with them for fear of dad's wrath if I tarnish myself–my skin–for my future wife.

Tidus' dad is nowhere near as strict as mine, and I've not told him that I'm looking down the barrel of an arranged marriage which is another reason I haven't pursued Rebekah or any other sexual escapades. I'm too afraid of the wrath of Giuseppe Capullo.

Going to uni for an art degree is enough of a rebellion, and he's letting me do that if I promise to marry whoever he chooses fit. It's my duty as the only son–the only child–to continue the Capullo name. A legacy that I really don't want to be a part of.

CHAPTER THREE

REECE

Dragging my suitcase behind me with one hand whilst holding my cat cage in the other I kick the door to my new university dorm room open. I'm thankful I managed to score a single room and don't have to share with someone who might realise who I am. It's going to be hard enough to keep a low profile as it is. To do my father's dirty work and not draw unwanted attention to myself.

My best friend Malyk pushes into the room, exuberant as usual. He leaps onto the bed, touching the roof with his palms as he jumps on the bed like a child.

"Nice and bouncy," he announces, as I put the cat cage down. "Good for fucking on."

I scoff at him. "Only you'd think and say that Mal."

CAZ MAY

He sits down on the bed, and I sit down next to him. He sniggers with a laugh, telling me, "You need to get laid, Ree."

I slap him on the side of the head. "Quit calling me that, dickhead."

My best friend has the gall to laugh at me again, teasing me, "Only if you quit calling me Mal."

"Not a chance," I taunt, smirking at him.

"Fine," he responds, still smirking when he asks, "So wanna test out the bed with me?"

"Again, not a chance, Mal." My tone is snide. Malyk knows I don't feel that way about him, but he can't help himself. It's just him.

"Fine," he huffs, sighing deeply and over the top. "A guy can only dream, and offer himself up so many times."

"I'm not losing you as my best mate because you want to fuck me, Malyk."

"I know. I know. I'll just dream until I find my guy."

I stand from the bed, and sit in the desk chair, spinning around on it.

"You still crushing on Tidus like an idiot?"

Malyk blushes, his gaze dropping from mine. "Yeah, I think the idiot is hot," he admits. I laugh a little, trying to hide it with a hand over my mouth. Malyk continues, "But he's a wanker."

I nod, confirming his words. "You don't have to tell me that. You could do so much better than Tidus Capullo."

Malyk chuckles, his smirk wide when he responds, "Yeah, true. But I'd fuck him any day. Hate sex and all."

"Hmmm," I mumble, wondering if the sex between me and Jasper would be hot if we got to fuck. I don't even know why I'm thinking that. Jasper is probably a heinous beast now. The cute guy turned ugly fucker.

"What're you mumbling about?"

"Oh nothing," I mumble again, spinning around the chair and looking down at the floor to hide the blush colouring my cheeks.

"It's not nothing that's got you blushing Ree."

I glance up at him, admitting softly, "I was thinking about Jasper."

Malyk chuckles but doesn't say anything.

"Wondering if he's hot now," I say, my cheeks darkening more to the point I can feel how hot they are.

"Oh he is," Malyk affirms, smiling at me. "But he's not gay my sweet."

"I know he's not. And I haven't seen him in years," I say. Malyk nods and I continue, "Plus we hate each other by default."

"Yeah, so back to this drab place," Malyk says, changing the subject.

"What?" I question, glancing around my new room. It's not the best space, but it's mine and for that I'm grateful.

"It needs the Malyk touch," he jeers.

"Do as you want, Mal," I tell him, adding with a laugh, "But no pink."

Malyk again chuckles, and scoffs, huffing his reply, "Never. Blasphemy." It was a taunt. My best friend is flamboyant and very openly gay in what could be seen as stereotypical to some and he has from time to time partaken in cross dressing. But he doesn't like overly girly things like the colour pink.

He's glancing around my room then, his eyes darting around as his mind ticks over with ideas. He can go and think about it. I need some space.

I stand from the chair, pushing it away and stalking towards him. Squaring my hands on his shoulders I hoist him up and he giggles at my touching him. He knows nothing is going to happen between us, but he still reacts to my touch and tries sometimes or teases me like he did earlier. I'm not going to give in to him. Fucking up our fifteen year friendship for sex is not worth it.

I shove him towards the door. "Alright, fuck off then. I'm beat."

I drop my hands from his shoulders, wrapping my arm around his waist to give him a side hug.

"Message received," he jeers as I step aside and open the door behind him. "You need a wank, and don't want me to watch," he says, smirking with his eyes grazing my body like he's thinking about watching me whilst I get off. I don't dignify that statement with an answer, instead, I push Malyk out the door, and he blows me kisses.

I shake my head in response, closing the door so hard it makes a whoosh sound. I flick the lock and bend down to the cat cage on the floor. My cat's loud meow reverberates around the small dorm room.

Opening the cage to get Raven out, I cradle him close and stroke his silky midnight black fur, shushing him.

"You'll have to be quiet here Rave," I tell him, his tiny ears pricking up as he looks up at me, and nudges against my chest. "People can't hear you meow, or they'll kick us out."

I put him down on the bed, and he immediately starts kneading the surface with his paws, claws out to make it soft and his. I know I'll have to hide him because I'm not supposed to have a cat in the dorms, but there was no way I was leaving him behind. Nothing beats stroking his fur, and listening to his purr when I'm all alone after a killing. It's the only other thing that calms the chaos in my head. Without Raven by my side–especially at night–I'd get no sleep. He lulls me to sleep with his purr and protects me from the demons that plague my head. He's my protector.

CHAPTER FOUR

Jasper

Slipping my arms into the crisp white dress shirt, I'm buttoning it up–and staring at myself in the mirror–when I'm startled by a knock on my bedroom door. I know who it is without even hearing her voice. My mother, coming to see if I'm dressed yet.

I don't want to go to this frat party organised by my parents at the university. It's not so much a frat party but a way for my parents to pretend they give a rats about my education, and to parade me and the next girl they're trying to set me up with. They've been trying to set me up with a wife–from another wealthy family–since the day I turned eighteen. And much to their annoyance–and disgust–I've turned down every one of them. All ten of them. And I've got no doubts I'll turn down this latest girl, even if she's the most gorgeous girl I've ever seen.

It's not that they're girls. I honestly couldn't care what gender they were, but it's the fact my parents are choosing for me. They're hypocrites. They were in love when they got married, and still are, madly so. It frustrates me that no matter how many times I tell them I want love, that I want to choose who I marry, they don't hear my plea. It's all about our wealth, our family name aligning with an equally wealthy family so the Capullo legacy lives on in Vemore.

"Jasper, dear, are you ready? May I come in?" she calls out through the door, opening it slightly even though I haven't answered her.

"Come in, Mother," I respond, continuing to button up my shirt and not turning to face her as she enters my bedroom.

"Are you wearing a tie, dear?" she asks, stepping up behind me and glaring at me in the mirror, a scowl on her face.

I shake my head, doing up the final button. "No mother," I tell her. "And if you request I do, I'm not leaving my room, let alone attending this farce of a party."

"How you wish, Jasper. Please finish dressing in haste. Your betrothed to be is waiting in the parlour."

I sigh, pouting, and turn to face her. "Don't pout, Jasper. It causes wrinkles."

She's always full of stupid advice like that. As if pouting causes wrinkles; more like smiling does. Mother is always smiling, and her face is wrinkled way more than it should be for a woman of less than fifty. She grips my waist and tucks my shirt in, yanking on the waistband of my slacks.

"Ouch, mother," I snap, shoving her hands away.

"You must look presentable. Miss London Devine is awaiting your presence."

Fuck me, even her name sounds pretentious. "Seriously, mother. I wish you'd stop this constant charade of setting me up. I want to find my love on my own."

"You will do nothing of the sort, Jasper. You will be marrying Miss London come spring."

I scoff. I want to spit words at her, angry words but I don't have it in me to hurt my mother. She'll be a sobbing mess and go to father which will earn me a talking to and a hiding to the backside, despite my being an adult capable of my own decisions.

I don't have a choice in this matter, so I need to suck it up and face my future wife.

"As you wish, Mother," I respond, following her out of my bedroom to the parlour.

A petite blonde girl is standing with her back to me, facing the fireplace. Her hands are clasped behind her back, and father is next to her speaking to her in hushed tones. Her dress is cream coloured, resembling a wedding dress of sorts, and I have to clear my throat to hide the scoff escaping my mouth. I hope I'm not actually going to be marrying her right now. I'd rather dive head first into the fireplace.

"Jasper, son," father says, his tone deep.

Miss London turns around to face us, and I have to admit she's pretty. Not breathtakingly so, but she has a classic simple beauty about her features.

"It's my pleasure to introduce Miss London Devine to you, as your newly betrothed."

I step closer to London, taking her hand and kissing the back of it.

"Miss London. It's a pleasure to make your acquaintance."

She curtsies to me, her delicate fingers clutching the side of her billowy dress.

"The pleasure is mine, Mr Capullo."

Her saying that formal greeting stabs my insides. I hate being called 'Mr'. It makes me feel like I'm my father, old and callous.

"Please if it's allowed I wish you to address me as Jasper." She nods at me, glancing a moment at Father who nods firmly, responding, "Allowed."

"As you wish, Jasper. You may call me London." I realise I'm still holding her hand, so I kiss it again.

"Are you ready to attend tonight's affair?"

"Most indeed, Jasper."

Still holding her hand, I lead her out of the parlour, and out to the limousine parked outside to take us to the party.

The chauffeur is holding the door open, and I continue holding London's hand as she slides inside before I follow.

She sighs, the door closing behind us.

"Thank goodness that's over," she muses, sighing again and smoothing the fabric of her dress over her thighs.

"Can I be frank with you London?"

"Of course Jasper."

"We won't be marrying."

She sighs again. "Thank goodness. I'm only here to appease my parents. I have a lover back in Hastings."

"Glad we're on the same page. Appease the parents for the night, and say we don't feel we're a suitable match."

"Sounds like a plan. Do you have a lover?"

Her choice of words—lover—strikes me as odd. It's formal, and not something someone our age usually says.

"No, I'm not seeing anyone. Not really interested in having a girlfriend."

"Oh, I'm not interested in a boyfriend either. Nadin is just a means to gain a release whilst dealing with the farce of my parents playing matchmakers."

I fall forward with the car stopping abruptly. My hands stop on her thighs.

"Sorry, I didn't mean to."

"It's ok. You may touch and kiss me as needed."

"I won't be doing anything like kisses."

"Oh, ok. Are you repulsed by me?"

"No, but you have someone in your life who you're involved with, and honestly I'm not interested in anything like that now. It's not you at all. I think you're pretty."

"Noted, you're not attracted to me."

"Exactly. Let's just try to enjoy the party, dance a little and move on."

She nods, and I take her hand again to help her out of the limo now that we've arrived at the party.

I can only hope this night is over quickly, and I can get back to the dorms. At least when I'm at university I'm free to be myself.

CHAPTER FIVE

REECE

Malyk is smiling like a giddy fool from the moment I open my dorm room door to him. I'm sure he's taken something, that he's high as fuck.

I shut the door behind him—so Rave doesn't escape—and he laughs like a crazed hyena.

"Ree, I have an invite for us."

"What in the hell are you on about, Mal?"

He yanks out a piece of paper from his pocket and waves it in my face.

"I got us an invite."

"To what?" I snap at him, annoyed. I snatch the piece of paper from him.

Capullo Frat Ball.
Valley View University commons
Friday 20th August
Beginning 8 pm

I scoff, shoving the invite against Malyk's chest.

"No fucking way, Mal. We're not going to a Capullo party."

"But we are, Ree. This invite summons us."

"Seriously Mal, you need to lay off the drugs."

He chuckles like the hyena again, his slender fingers again delving inside his pocket. Withdrawing them on his fingertip he has a small round ecstasy tablet. He holds it out to me. "Take it, Ree." I want to protest, but Malyk won't stand for that. His idea of fun is getting high and drunk and then fucking a random stranger. I'm down for the latter. It's been way too long since I've been with a guy. I know I could take Malyk up on his offer of a quick fuck, but his feelings for me make that a no-go. Plus he doesn't even get a rise out of my dick. He's my best friend. Nothing more. Ever.

"Reece, you gonna take the little fun time pill?" he taunts me, pressing it against my lips with a smirk on his face.

I don't respond but stick out my tongue and Malyk puts the tiny pill into my mouth. I take it in and he lets his finger linger in my mouth as I close my lips around the digit. Malyk groans which pisses me off, so I bite down hard on his finger and he yanks it out of my mouth, rubbing at the mark I made on his knuckle.

"You bit me, Ree."

"Had to get your dirty finger out of my mouth somehow, Mal. You were enjoying that way too much."

"Can't help it. I was thinking about your stunning lips wrapped around my cock."

"Not going to happen, Mal. Ever. You need to find another guy to suck you off."

He laughs, less like a hyena but still nerve grating. "Maybe you'll find a guy tonight. Get you laid."

I scoff, swallowing hard before replying, "I don't want a guy, Malyk."

"Don't want, but need my sweet. There is a difference."

"Whatever, Mal. Are we going to this party or getting high here?"

"Partying up the night. And make sure you stick by my side for the most part. We don't want Capullo wankers recognising you."

I nod, grabbing my hoodie from the back of my chair and shrugging it on.

Bending down I stroke Raven's head a moment, and he jumps up on the bed behind me. "Be good Rave," I instruct him, stroking his fur a little more as he gets comfortable on my pillow. "No loud meowing."

He doesn't respond. I follow Malyk out then, ignoring his scathing gaze about my outfit choice of black, ripped at the knees jeans and my favourite black hoodie with white writing on it that doesn't make any sense.

We really shouldn't have driven since both of us are high, but the cops don't give a rats' arse around Vemore about cars literally flying around the streets.

Braking hard, I careen around the last corner to park outside Valley View University. There are so many cars, and I can already hear the thump of music coming from inside the university commons.

Malyk drags me out of the car, not even giving me a moment to pocket my phone and barely a moment to turn off the engine and pocket my key fob. He takes my hand, dragging me through the ornate gates of the university. The music grows louder and I can feel the thump in my head, the vibrations increasing the intensity of my high.

Once in the commons, I glance around, taking in the party scene around us. There are bodies everywhere, some dressed in plain clothes and others in drag costumes. That strikes me as odd, but then I don't really care. My high is starting to hit, and my whole body feels alive with the buzz. Malyk drops my hand, and whispers in my ear, "Be a good boy, Ree. I gotta schmooze with the invitees."

I hear his words but don't really process them. He dances off into the crowd, and I wander further into the party, my eyes taking in more of the space, drawn to the stage when I see my best friend dancing onto it. I have to be super high, surely seeing things because not only is Malyk on stage but he's decked out in a full drag outfit, complete with feathers in his tied-back hair and fishnet fucking stockings. Admittedly he looks hot, and I'm mesmerised for a moment watching him strutting around the stage to 'I Will Survive' in his over the top, exuberant way.

Throwing my own body around on the dance floor I occasionally glance at others once Malyk is no longer on the stage. My high is wearing off too quickly so I head to the bar and order a beer.

Leaning against the bar top I scout the room again. I'd said to Malyk I wasn't going to find a guy tonight, but I can't deny that I do need to get laid. I spot a guy across the room. A gorgeous blonde dancing with a girl. His arms are wrapped around her waist, and hers are around his neck. They're swaying to the slow song playing through the speakers. He looks as though he'd rather be anywhere else, his expression vacant. I can't take my eyes off him.

The song ends, and they step apart, him nodding at her and she does a fucking curtsy, as though we're living in the nineteenth century and this is actually a ball, not a frat party.

I watch the stranger as he comes my way, his eyes on me but not actually looking at me, but kinda through me. He turns at the last moment, heading towards the bathrooms. I shouldn't even be entertaining the thought of following him because he's most likely not gay, and following anyone into the bathrooms is creepy, but I put my empty glass down on the bar top and head to the bathrooms.

They're empty except for the gorgeous stranger who is washing his hands at the sinks. I stand behind him, and our eyes lock in the mirror.

"Excuse me," he says, his voice a little shy and raspy. Fucking sexy as hell.

"Don't mind me, gorgeous," I reply, stepping closer to him rather than away from him.

"Do you mind?"

"Not at all," I taunt, snaking an arm around his waist and pushing him against the wall. He moves without a protest, except for a gasp escaping his lips.

"Um…what are you doing?"

"I saw you on the dance floor."

"Um…ok…and…"

"It looked like you weren't having a good time."

"I wasn't…and I'm not now."

"Maybe I can change your mind, gorgeous," I taunt him again, gripping his perfectly angled jaw. He gasps again and I chuckle slightly before I yank him closer to crash our lips together. His lips are soft and smooth and fit with mine like a perfect match. His lips on mine are igniting a fire from within. He's reluctant to kiss me back, so I break the kiss and increase the pressure of my grip on his jaw.

"Don't you kiss back?"

"I…don't…kiss strangers."

"You already did gorgeous, so kiss me again and I'll no longer be a stranger."

He gasps again, and fuck it's sexy. He's sexy. My dick is pulsing in my jeans and I slide my other hand into his blonde waves, tugging on the strands to pull him closer for another kiss. He moans this time, kissing me back and involuntarily darting his tongue out to lick the bow of my lips. I groan at that, pushing my pelvis against his. I can feel his dick brushing against mine, our kiss turning frantic with bites of our lips and our tongues playing. I feel weightless and I never want to come up for air, to break this kiss.

My bliss is cut short though, when the door squeals open behind us. I step away from the stranger who's panting for breath and staring at me and then to who is behind us. I turn to find my best friend standing there with a hand on his hip, his expression near irate. He grabs my hand, forcefully pulling me away and out of the bathroom.

"Seriously Mal. You tell me to hook up and then you dare interrupt."

He pulls me aside even more, into the dark hallway away from the party.

I eye him annoyed. "You jealous I wasn't kissing you?"

"No, Reece. Do you not know who you were just kissing?"

I shake my head, unfazed. "No, but surely he was just a hot as hades stranger."

Malyk shakes his head, scoffing. "Not a stranger…but the son of our enemy, Jasper Capullo."

I gasp, touching my kiss swollen lips. I can still feel his kiss. "You're shitting me?"

Malyk shakes his head even more violently than before. "I shit you not my friend."

"Fuck," I curse, before asking Mal, "How did he get so gorgeous?"

"He grew up, and came into himself." He certainly had grown up. No longer the ugly duckling but fuck...a gorgeous fuckable swan that can kiss a man like it's not a sin.

"I can see that. But fuck, Mal. I kissed him. I kissed Jasper Capullo, my sworn enemy."

Malyk laughs, and I elbow him in the side. "And what shall you do about it?" He taunts.

"Slap my best mate silly for talking like a dufus and then..." I contemplate my words, wondering what I do want to actually do now that I've kissed my enemy.

Malyk taunts me more, "And then what?"

I glare at him and respond, "Find Jasper to sin again, because that kiss was the best damn kiss of my life."

Malyk sniggers. "That may be easier than you think."

"What do you know, you devil?" I ask in a mocking tone.

"That our dear Jasper has just moved into the Valley View University dorms."

I kiss Malyk's cheek. He giggles, and I nearly slap him for that reaction before I respond with a snide tone, "Hmm. I guess he's going to get a visit."

Malyk doesn't respond then. He knows nothing will change my mind when I'm set on what I want. It's probably going to be my demise, but I want Jasper Capullo—my sworn enemy—and I always get what I want.

CHAPTER SIX

Jasper

The moment after the stranger left the bathroom I snuck out completely on edge, glancing every which way hoping no one saw. I don't even stop to speak to anyone, leaving the party to walk back to the dorms.

I'm barely a metre away from the commons when I hear footsteps behind me. Clanking footsteps that can only be made by platform sneakers. I only know of one person who wears that kind of stupid shoes.

My best friend Nancy. I slow my pace but don't turn to look at her. She stops beside me, matching my steps, puffing. I stop dead and she bumps into me.

"Jasp, what are you doing walking out here in the dark?"

I can't look at her. Looking at her will cause all the emotions tearing me up inside to pour out. I

CAZ MAY

can't hide my emotions, especially from Nancy. She'll see right through me.

"Jasp, you're scaring me," she says exasperated. "Did something happen at the party?"

I shake my head, a sob escaping my lips as I turn to look at her, pulling her into a hug. Her voice is muffled into my shoulder, "Jasp, please tell me what's wrong?"

Even though I want to continue hugging her for comfort, I pull back.

"I kissed someone at the party," I admit, feeling my cheeks colouring.

Nancy's eyes light up. "Your newly betrothed?"

Again I shake my head and start walking off again. Nancy follows me, her steps matching mine.

"No, it was a guy," I confess, turning away from her gaze so she doesn't see my cheeks heating, remembering his kiss.

"A guy? You kissed a guy?" Nancy questions, her tone intrigued.

"Yeah," I respond, kicking the rocks underfoot. "Well, he kissed me."

"And?" Nancy replies, her tone almost snide.

"And what, Nanc?"

"Was it a good kiss?" she probes for more. I ponder her question, reliving the kiss in my mind, trying not to groan at the memory of the pleasure I felt with his lips on mine.

"Amazing. I didn't know kisses could feel like that."

"Hmm, so who was this guy?"

I shrug. "I didn't get his name. One of the dancer guys pulled him away and seemed angry at him."

"Oh," Nancy stammers, shocked and stopping dead as we walk into common grounds surrounding the dorms. "What did he look like?" she blurts out, adding, "The guy you kissed I mean."

"Dark messy hair and covered in tattoos," I answer, sighing when I add, "And mesmerising grey eyes."

Nancy gasps. "You said the dancer knew him?"

"I'm guessing so, why do you ask?"

"It could only be one."

I give her an incredulous puzzled look. "Who Nanc?"

"Reece," she mumbles, surveying the ground instead of meeting my eyes.

"Montserrat?" I question flatly, hoping her answer is no.

But of course, I couldn't be so lucky, as my best friend responds to explain, "Yes, the main dancer tonight was Malyk Exton. They're best friends, Jasp."

I shake my head violently, collapsing onto a stone seat in the courtyard with my head in my hands as I try to hold back my tears.

"Oh god, Nancy! I kissed a Montserrat," I screech, my voice and breathing wheezy.

Nancy sits beside me, a hand on my knee.

"Don't worry about it Jasp. I'm sure no one other than Malyk saw it."

I eye her then. "I hope so, Nanc. Because no one can know I kissed the enemy."

"I won't tell a soul," she promises, before questioning me, "but Jasp?"

"Yeah?" I mumble, quirking my eyebrow up.

"Do you want to kiss him again?"

"I'd be lying if I said no," I admit, trying to hide the smile that wants to cross my face. "But I'll do nothing to cause kissing him again to come to fruition."

"If that's what you wish, Jasp. I just want you to be happy."

"And I am Nanc. I'm here at university to study art history. It's all I want."

"Ok, well goodnight then dear friend," Nancy says standing from the seat as I do. We kiss each other's cheeks in turn and I reply, "Goodnight my dear Nancy."

After Nancy walks off with a wave I head to my dorm room, and fall back on my bed, sighing exasperated.

I can't believe I kissed Reece Montserrat and enjoyed it; loved it quite frankly. No kiss has ever felt that arousing–not that I've had many–but I know it was beyond amazing. I'm annoyed at myself that I still can't stop thinking about how Reece's lips felt on mine and that my dick is stirring in my underwear, reliving the kiss in my mind as I drift off to sleep. Kissing the enemy was a sin enough, but still thinking about it is giving into the devil's temptations–my desires–that I've been hiding inside. I shouldn't want to sin again with Reece –or any guy– but after kissing the enemy I'm thinking about sinning in ways far more naughty than kissing. Reece Monserrat is the devil in the flesh.

CHAPTER SEVEN

REECE

t's dusk when I go to Jasper's uni, Valley View University or Capullo family old as shit university. It's a legacy university and you can barely set foot in the place if you're not affiliated with the Capullo family.

They don't know me though. I'm a criminal from the wrong side of the city, Montserrat territory and I can find my way in anywhere and take down whoever I need to that gets in my way in the process of getting what I want.

The external doors are open, so I head inside without a hitch. I have my hoodie on and tug on the strings to pull it around my face. Taking notice of all the overhead signage I tiptoe down the hallways, not making eye contact with anyone until I get to the Dean's office. It's locked–as I suspected. From the pocket at the front of my hoodie, I grab out my black woollen gloves, slipping them on and wiping the handle to rid it of my fingerprints. I'd also stashed some alcohol wipes in my pocket, so I grab one of those out and wipe the door handle as well. I'm resourceful like that. Can't leave a trail that would have the cops on my back, even though I quite literally get away with murder so a simple break and enter would be nothing but a blip on the radar as far as I'm concerned.

I grab the bobby pin I've stashed out of my pocket, slip it into the lock and shift it around in the lock until the mechanism clicks and the knob turns in my gloved hand. Once in the Dean's office, I check his drawers for a key to the filing cabinet, almost instantly finding one because the Dean is such a predictable fucker. Opening the filing cabinet I rummage through his files to find out the details of Jasper's room.

Practically everything I need to know about Jasper Capullo is in the file. His family deets, his birthday, GPA, and his course of study. I laugh at his course choice. Fucking Art History. That's going to get him so far in life. Not. Fucking idiot.

But I'm not concerned with his life story. I just need his room number, which is on yet another piece of paper. I snavel that, folding it and shoving it in my hoodie pocket for future reference since I know I won't remember it the moment I step out of

CAZ MAY

this room. My memory is like a sieve sometimes. It holds onto memories and things I'd rather forget, and I can't remember things I'd like–and need–to.

Putting the file back in its spot, I close the filing cabinet and lock it before putting the key back in the exact spot I got it from.

For a moment I think about ransacking the office to show I've been there, but I don't bother wasting anymore time. The Dean won't even know I've been here, so it's unnecessary.

I lock and close the door behind me, and sneak down the hallway towards the dorm. I keep my hoodie on and am annoyed at how many people are around in the hallways. I hope no one recognises me.

Getting to Jasper's door, I check the paper to make sure I'm at the right door. I'm tempted to kick it down. But I know that's not wise. I exhale a deep breath, about to knock when the door careens open. I fall forward pushing Jasper back into his room as he's coming out.

Sniggering, I kick the door closed behind me. Jasper gasps, his face turning ashen.

"Jasper Capullo," I tease with a rasp. "Fancy seeing you here."

He scoffs. "What are you doing here Reece?"

"Coming to see you," I holler, still with the same smoky tone in my voice.

"You shouldn't be here. If someone sees you your death is guaranteed."

I laugh at him. "My blood would be on your hands Jasper," I respond, raspy right in his face.

"I'm not going to kill you, Reece," Jasper confesses. "Even if you're a Montserrat and I hate you." He's seething, the word 'hate' sounding like he's injecting me with a dose of poison.

"I hate you too, Jasper," I spit at him in a snide voice.

We stare at each other then, breathing heavily. His lustful gaze on me is causing my dick to strain in my jeans. Fuck. I want him so bad. He's fucked me over with just a couple of kisses.

"Fuck it," I rasp, gripping Jasper's neck, yanking him forward for a kiss. He resists for a moment, but when I lick his lips to demand entrance Jasper gives in, moaning against my mouth as the kiss deepens. Jasper's arms wrap around my waist pulling me even closer as we kiss. It's euphoric. His kisses take me somewhere else, to another time and space where we can be together and aren't enemies. Our bodies are grinding against each other. Jasper's dick is hardening, as is mine. He groans and breaks the kiss.

"Damn Capullo, seems you like kissing me."

"I don't. I hate you," Jasper hisses, biting down on his kiss swollen lip.

"You might hate me but your body doesn't," I taunt, nodding towards Jasper's obvious erection.

"Reflex. My body is a traitor."

"Hmm. I beg to differ, Jasper."

"I hate you, Reece," he drawls out, shoving me aside enraged.

"Leaving so soon? I just got here, Jasp."

Jasper seethes, hissing at me, "Don't call me that."

He's so striking when he's mad. "And yes I'm leaving for the dining hall. Supper is served at six pm, and I'm already late."

I scoff. This place is pretentious. "They seriously serve you here in a fucking dining hall?"

"Yes, and I'm late, so please leave," Jasper remarks, opening the door and holding it open, gesturing for me to leave. I can't help but notice the pulsing veins in his rather large hands, his long fingers that I desperately want to feel on every inch of my skin.

"Well, I was planning to stay here and wait for you to come back for more kisses but since you said please..." I pause, my voice trailing off and I laugh at Jasper's rising chest, his breaths audible showing he's seething and trying to keep his cool. To stay calm in my presence, which admittedly turns me on more than it probably should.

"Leave now!"Jasper rages, stomping his foot.

"Ooo, there's my Jasp," I taunt.

He groans in an irritated way, shoving me out the door before slamming it behind him. With his hands on my chest, he's pushing me down the hallway. I love his hands on me.

"Don't call me Jasp, and don't come here again, Reece," he says, way too loudly considering the hallway is full of students. "I'll report you to the dean."

I snicker. "Ooo, I love you manhandling me, Jasp."

He scoffs, withdrawing his hands and stepping aside a little. His mouth opens as though he wants to respond but no words come out, so I continue, "And do your worst. The dean of this shithole university doesn't scare me."

Jasper blushes slightly, then turns away and heads down the opposite end of the hallway without a word. I'm still stunned, standing there in a fucking daze. When Jasper is halfway down the hallway he turns back to face me, giving me an up yours. His slender finger outstretched like that is a tease he doesn't even realise he's taunting me with. I can't help but think about what that very finger would feel like caressing my insides—teasing my spot—whilst he's stroking my dick.

I laugh, adjusting my dick in my jeans. Jasper has pushed me away, but there's no way I'm going to be able to keep away now I've had another taste of him, and he's shown his fiery side. He says he hates me—and I feel the same way—but there's a fine line between love and hate. Whilst I don't believe in love, I do believe in lust. And Jasper Capullo—my sworn enemy—stirs up a hunger in me I've never felt before. I crave him.

CHAPTER EIGHT

Jasper

Walking out of class I kiss Nancy on the cheek goodbye as usual. She walks off, giving me a wave and I feel a shiver rush through me—one of those someone walking over your grave ones—even though it's not cold today with the sun shining. I feel like someone is watching me. I glance around the buildings and courtyard but can't see anyone nearby who's looking at me.

I start walking down the cobbled stone pathway towards the student centre to get some more art supplies for my project. It's nice being outside on such a nice day and I sigh, inhaling the warm air as I pass under the archway into the tree-lined pathway. I'm still feeling cold, and brush the goosebumps on my arms to try and warm myself up. Still, I continue glancing around—hitching the strap of my backpack higher on my shoulder and clutching it tight—because I feel uneasy.

Abruptly I stop in my tracks at a large oak tree, sure I can hear someone breathing heavily. It's probably stupid to check it out but I step onto the grass and I'm pulled aside. I gasp, coming face to face with someone I didn't think I'd be seeing so soon, or at all again after he came into my room the other day.

"Reece."

"Avoiding me huh, Jasp?"

"No. Well, yes," I stammer, as I try to walk away. I don't have the chance to move even an inch because Reece grips my arm and yanks me closer. So close I'm standing in between his parted legs, so close I could kiss him. And I want to kiss him, but I don't make the move.

"You enjoyed art class today? Painting that naked dude?" he questions me, his eyes darkening. No wonder I felt as though someone was watching me during class too. He was there, in the background.

"No. I'd rather it was a girl," I answer, gulping down the lump in my throat. My answer isn't truthful.

"Really? You don't think the naked male form is sexy, Jasp?" he enquires raspy with a wicked smirk on his face.

"No Reece," I respond feeling myself blush. "I don't." Again I'm lying—kinda—as I find most nakedness attractive in some way. I think the naked body is a beautiful art form, but I'm not going to give Reece any satisfaction of knowing that about me. I'm not going to give him any indication of my sexuality. I'm still unsure of what my sexuality is. Sometimes I think I'm bisexual, and then other times I feel I'm pansexual.

Reece chuckles. "The colour of your cheeks shows your lies, Jasp." His voice still has that rasp, and I hate–and love–how the annoying nickname sounds falling from his lips yet again.

"Stop, stop calling me that."

"Why? You like it, Jasp."

I groan, shoving him in the chest to push him away as I scream, "Stop!"

"Make me, Jasp," he hisses, then he groans and taunts as he leans in closer, "Shut me up with your mouth."

I grip his t-shirt in a fist. "You wish. I hate you."

"Well, Jasper," Reece taunts, eyeballing me. "I crave you. And I've never craved anything until I tasted your kiss."

I shake my head, still beholding his gaze. "You don't deserve to kiss me. You can't go around taking what you want, Reece."

"You say that like I want you, Jasper," he jibs, his tone inept.

"Well, don't you?" I question, kicking myself in the guts for such an eager response. He'll see right through my bravado. See that I—quite stupidly—want him.

Reece shakes his head. "No. I hate you, Jasper." His voice is hoarse, and I moan. Reece grips my neck, and yanks me closer, crushing my lips to his.

Inwardly, I curse myself as I give into Reece's kiss again. He pushes into me, our dicks both hardening and brushing against each other causing pulse racing friction. Groaning, I pull back, breaking the kiss in preparation of raising my hand to slap it across Reece's cheek. He hisses at the contact of my palm.

"You can't kiss me like that," I thunder at him, adding slightly calmer, "Here."

Reece smirks and chuckles, gripping my wrist. I fight with myself to continue staring at him. I want to look away but I can't turn my gaze from his.

"Your kisses are like a hit of the most illicit drug, Capullo. You can't keep denying how much you love my kiss on your pretty mouth, Jasp."

"I...I...hate you," I stutter, wrenching my wrist out of his grip. "Leave me alone, Reece!"

He laughs again. "Feelings mutual, Jasp," he insists, smirking again.

I huff, picking up my backpack I'd dropped when Reece gripped my arm. I trudge away and flip Reece off again. I hear him groan and moan behind me, and hate that it causes my dick to stir in my jeans.

Not looking back, I head to the student centre. Once there I quickly select the brushes, canvas and paints I need for class. Plonking them down on the counter, I give the girl a coy smile.

"Is this all for today?"

"Yes, thanks."

"Do you like painting portraits or full bodies?" she asks, smiling at me.

I don't know why she's trying to engage me in a conversation, especially as there's a hint of flirtation in her voice, her gaze roaming my body.

"Ah, both I guess. We're doing full bodies in class at the moment."

"Maybe you'll get to paint me some time then. I volunteer as a model."

"Maybe," I reply, my tone flat. I don't feel anything for her. There's no attraction for this pretty girl. I'd have rather seen London naked and I wasn't attracted to her either. I can't stop thinking about Reece. For some unbeknownst reason, that dickhead is the only person my body seems to have taken a liking to lately. I don't want to be attracted to the enemy, yet I am. I pay for my items, shoving them in my backpack—the canvas tucked under my arm—and I leave, running back to my dorm to shower in the hope of washing away the sin tarnishing me from kissing Reece. I know it's essentially a sin, except it doesn't feel like a sin with him. I'm going to hell. My sins will send me under.

CHAPTER NINE

REECE

*H*aving snuck around the Valley View campus a few times now I've worked out exactly where Jasper's room is, which window is his. It's dark now–past eight–so he'll be back from supper and hopefully in his dorm room.

Picking up a few rocks from the ground I pelt them at the window. It's drawing attention to myself but no one is around.

After having thrown three smaller rocks without a response I edge closer to the window, and bang on it with my palm, speaking in a low voice, "Jasper."

It seems like a lifetime when he finally slides the window open and glares at me annoyed.

"What're you doing here, Reece?" he questions, his tone snarky.

"Coming to see you. What else would I be doing?"

"Did anyone see you?"

"So what if they did," I remark, smirking at him.

"I care, Reece. People can't see us together." I laugh at his stupidity, gripping his hands on the window sill.

"Well, then let me in, Jasp."

"Why would I let you into my room again?" he observes, raising his eyebrow.

"Because you want me."

"Do not. I hate you."

"So you keep saying, but you haven't exactly pushed me away, Jasp." He scoffs and steps back from the window. I slip–losing my footing a moment–before I hoist myself up on the window ledge to crawl inside his room. His bed is there so I land on it–on my arse–with a thud. He's standing beside the bed, arms folded over his chest.

"I don't want you here, Reece."

I stand, climbing off his bed and shoving him against the wardrobe. "Tell me to go then, Jasper."

He gasps then, a whimper escaping his lips when I grip the front of his t-shirt, tugging him closer.

"I hate you," he hisses at me, licking his lips, his tongue swiping across the deep bow of his lips.

"Mmm, I hate you too, Jasp," I say before crashing my lips to his for a hard kiss. He moans into the kiss, and I pull back. "You can't deny you love kissing me, Jasp."

"I don't. I could be kissing anyone and I'd react the same way," he protests, his cheeks colouring with a blush that contradicts his words. He loves kissing me, and only me. Reaching down between us, I grip his hardening cock. "Maybe so, but I'm the only one who causes your cock to harden."

He shakes his head, moaning as I begin stroking his cock over the front of his pyjama pants.

"Mmm, Reece," he murmurs. "That…feels… so…good."

Groaning, I continue stroking his cock, kissing him again and demanding entrance to fuck his mouth by biting down on his lower lip. The bite draws blood, and he licks it away, lacing his tongue with mine so I can taste the blood too. And fuck. Fuck. That turns me on. My dick instantly hardens, tenting my sweats and kissing Jasper harder I piston my hips forward so my dick is brushing against his. The contact–the friction–causes him to groan and he breaks the kiss with a loud moan, and a breathy, "Fuck."

I gasp and grip his waist to push him down onto the bed. "You turn me on, so damn much, Capullo."

Again he groans and grips my neck to pull me down for a kiss. I fucking love this feisty side of him. Jasper is shy—most of the time—outside the bedroom but he lets loose when he's in my arms and takes everything my dominant side requests of him. We kiss for a while, all moans and groans, tongues battling and teeth clashing. I could kiss Jasper Capullo twenty-four fucking seven for eternity and it would never be enough. Damn him.

I break the kiss however because I need more. More kisses. More touching, skin on skin.

"Jasp," I murmur, gulping before continuing with a more authoritative tone, "Get naked."

He shakes his head at me. "No," he snaps, licking his lips.

"I said get naked, Capullo."

He stares at me, his eyebrows furrowing. "Not happening, Reece."

"You like playing games, Jasper?"

"No. I just don't get naked in front of people I don't know."

I scoff. "I've had my tongue down your throat and touched your damn dick in your pj pants, Jasp."

"So, that means nothing."

"Right, so you go around letting every guy you meet kiss and touch you?"

He blushes then, shifting a little under me so he's sitting up against the headboard.

He again shakes his head. "No, you're the only guy I've kissed. And no one, not even a girl has touched me that way." His cheeks are a deep crimson.

"Fuck, Capullo. You're killing me."

He licks his lips again, mumbling, "I'm sorry."

"Don't give me that shit. Seriously, just get naked."

He nods, grabbing the hem of his t-shirt and pulling it over his head. He throws it on the floor, and I admire his body for a moment. He's ripped, a long deep ridge defining his abs. "Fuck Jasper. You're ripped."

"Ah, thanks," he mumbles, his shyness showing again with his blush.

"Take your pants off," I demand, staring at him. He shakes his head, and fuck if his defiance doesn't turn me on.

"Only if you strip first."

"Doesn't work that way with me, Jasp," I taunt him, gripping the waistband of his pj pants, and yanking them down to free his hard dick. I gasp eyeing his hard length, already glistening with precum.

He wiggles out of the pants as I pull them down further, shuffling back down on the bed so I can pull them off him completely.

"Your body and cock are a work of art, Jasper," I remark, leaning back over him to kiss him hard.

He moans against my lips on his, writhing his hips beneath me. "More…more…Reece..please…" he rasps, his breath fanning my face as he breaks the kiss.

"More? You want more?"

"Yes, please," he pants, gripping the front of my t-shirt. Brushing his hand away I pull my t-shirt off and stand a moment to discard my sweats and boxers. My dick is so hard it's pointing straight at Jasper when I climb back onto the bed.

"Oh, wow. You're huge," he comments, his gaze lingering on my dick which causes it to jerk in response.

"Yeah, touch me, Jasper."

"I…I've…never."

"Fucking touch me, Capullo," I demand, clutching his wrist and pulling his hand towards my aching cock. He wraps his long delicate fingers around my length, hesitating.

He bites down on his lip, unsure of what to do next. "Have you never stroked a damn dick before, Capullo?"

He shakes his head. "No."

"Never?"

Again he shakes his head, not replying but his answer is a clear no and I can't help but scoff.

Seems like Jasper is a virgin or maybe he's just playing me because no guy as gorgeous as him our age is that pure.

"Fuck, Capullo. I knew you were innocent, but fuck me dead I didn't think you were that pure."

"I guess you don't want me now," he responds, his cheeks colouring again.

I snigger. "I want you even more, Jasper."

"Oh, um…" he mumbles, biting down on his lip and taking his hand back. I want to say something snarky but instead, I clasp his dick in my fist and start to slowly stroke his length, whilst watching his eyes that are caught with mine.

We don't exchange words, just stare at each other as I coat his glorious uncut dick with his precum as lube. He can't help but buck his hips up, moans beginning to escape his lips as the pleasure builds.

"Oh, shit…Reece!" he bellows, his dick jerking and his hips bucking off the bed as he comes all over his stomach and my hand. I smear it over his skin–and lick my hand–still watching him. His face twists in disgust.

"Fuck, you taste divine, Jasp."

"Really?" he questions, his eyebrow quivering.

"Divine, Capullo," I taunt, bending down to lave my tongue over the come on his stomach until his light claire skin is clean. I don't stop licking his body though, then trailing my tongue into that deep ridge of his abs, all the way up his body until I kiss his lips once more.

Immediately he turns the kiss feral, flitting his tongue over my lips to taste himself on them. I'm about to break the kiss when his hands find my cheeks, and he's yanking me closer, the kiss deepening to the point it feels as though my lips will be bruised. His kiss is punishing and fuck I'm here for it. He lets out a loud groan, breaking the kiss suddenly as he roars, "Oh god, fuck Reece!"

I pull back, realising I've just come all over him without even a touch. And he too has come again.

I could be embarrassed by my pubescent ejaculation but it's the opposite. No one has ever made me come without a touch, with just a kiss. Until now. Until Jasper Capullo. My sworn enemy.

"Damn, Capullo. Your hot as fuck kisses made me come."

"Oh, um. I'm sorry."

"Fuck off with the sorry, dickhead. I didn't say it was a bad thing."

"Oh, ok," he mumbles, again biting down on his plump lip.

I laugh, slipping a finger into the come covering my dick. I put it to his lips.

"Open, Jasp. Taste my come."

He shakes his head, biting his lip harder.

"Come on, Jasper. You're gonna taste my come and fucking love it."

He still doesn't open his mouth, so I scoop up more come, smearing it all over his lips, and his deep philtrum.

He gasps for breath and then, involuntarily licks his lips. His eyes light up and he smiles, licking his lips again, his tongue laving over them multiple times as he groans.

"Taste good, Jasp?"

"Yeah, it does actually," he comments, licking his lips again for any lingering come. I run my fingers through the come on his stomach again and slip the finger into his mouth. His tongue swoops over it, and he sucks on it until it's clean. I withdraw it with a pop, and taunt him, "Next time you're going to do that with your pretty lips wrapped around my cock instead, until I'm coming down your throat and you swallow every last drop."

He gasps, his eyes going wide at my suggestion.

"There won't be a next time, Reece."

I laugh, and stand up from the bed, pulling on my sweats–sans boxers.

"Oh yes there fucking will be, Capullo," I taunt as I tug on my t-shirt.

Leaning over I give him one last kiss–for now– not letting him turn it to a fierce one before I stumble towards the door and leave without a word from either of us.

If tonight was anything to go by, being with Jasper Capullo is going to kill me.

We'd gotten off together, and I'm craving more. Craving his kisses. Craving his touch. And craving–aching to, dying to–fuck his damn brains out.

I knew before being with him that I like to be dominant in the bedroom, but his little bratty moments nearly sent me over the edge and I want to dominate him by fucking him so hard he'll see stars and crave me as much I crave him.

Fuck, I'm fucked up for my enemy.

CHAPTER TEN

Jasper

Sitting in the common room, I'm staring absentmindedly at the sandwich in my hand. Nancy is sitting beside me, munching on her own sandwich. I like that even though she doesn't–isn't allowed to–attend Valley View she can still come hang out to have lunch with me.

Today I'm feeling out of sorts, still thinking about what I did last night–in my dorm room–with Reece. With a Montserrat and a guy at that. I let him see me naked, let him kiss me, and touch me until I committed the ultimate sin. I gave into the temptation–and felt the sin of pleasure–multiple times. Nancy must notice my off mood. She gulps down a bite of her sandwich, asking abruptly, "Jasp, are you ok?"

"Um…yes…no," I stammer, taking a big bite of my sandwich so I don't have to say anything for a moment whilst I collect my thoughts.

"Jasp, you can tell me anything," Nancy prompts.

I lift my gaze to hers, responding, "I know. It's just that I did something bad."

"How bad?"

"Well, Reece snuck into my room last night and we kissed again."

"That isn't bad, Jasp. Did something else happen?"

I nod, taking another bite of my sandwich. I can't believe I'm about to admit to my sins, to actually voice them to my best friend.

"We...um...got naked," I begin, feeling my cheeks heating with the confession. Nancy gasps but doesn't utter a single word.

"And then he touched me...my penis...and I gave into the pleasure until I had an orgasm... twice."

Again Nancy gasps, and then giggles with her question, "Did you like it?"

"Yeah, Nanc, but I shouldn't," I admit, trying to stop my mind from wandering back.

"Why?"

"Because it's a sin," I respond, shaking my head. "Doing those things with a guy."

"Who says?" Nancy snaps, balling her fists as though she wants to beat up someone for filling my mind with the knowledge of sin.

"My parents, the church. God."

She laughs, shaking her head animatedly. "Jasp, it's the 21st damn century. Who cares?" She's not wrong. We don't live in the dark ages. But I still care about doing the right thing.

"Me, Nanc. I care."

"You shouldn't," my best friend responds, adding with a smile, "Love who you love."

I scoff, taking a final bite of my sandwich and a sip of coffee that I forgot was even on the table in front of me. It's tepid so doesn't taste very appetising, but I take a few more sips before responding to Nancy with a snip in my voice, "I don't love Reece. I hate him."

Nancy laughs. "Hate is also a sin, Jasp. Some say it is one of the deadly sins."

Panic rises in my chest and I gulp hard. "So you're saying I'm going to hell regardless?"

"No, Jasper. But you can't live life in this world chained to the past teachings. Things are not as they were when the church ruled." Again she's showing she's wise beyond her years.

"I know, Nanc. But I can't just let go of all I've been taught, of all I know," I tell her, finishing my coffee. I'm ready to leave, to check out from this conversation but Nancy's glare pins me to the spot still.

"That is but true Jasp. But you need to trust your heart. It won't steer you wrong."

"My heart is not of a concern when it comes to Reece," I sneer and again Nancy laughs as though she's mocking me.

"Don't be so sure. Our bodies are governed by our hearts."

"Need you talk in riddles, Nanc," I chastise her annoyed. Nancy is wise and knowledgeable in regard to history, but sometimes her words confuse me.

"Just think about it Jasper," she instructs, reaching out to touch my hand on the table. "And listen to your heart. Let it guide your hand in painting your heart's desire."

I don't respond but stand from the table now we've finished lunch. I smile at my best friend, and air kiss her cheeks before going to art class.

Sitting in front of my canvas, holding up the brush against the taut fabric I'm breathing heavily in concentration. Our instructions for the class were to paint with our minds' eye. To not think too hard about what we're painting and just let the brush do the talking.

To achieve this I close my eyes, moving my brush in slow strokes over the canvas. Whilst painting I softly hum a tune, and I don't even open my eyes as I dip my brush into the paints beside me. It's odd just letting go, and painting without seeing what's on the canvas, or even what colours I'm using. It's freeing. And it's causing my heart to beat erratically in an exhilarating way like it does when I'm with Reece.

The class goes by quickly, and when the professor announces for paint brushes down I flutter my eyes open and stare at my work. I've painted a face. And studying it I realise it looks exactly like Reece. I need to stop thinking about him and stop letting him into my dorm room to taunt me, to tempt me to sin.

CAZ MAY

CHAPTER ELEVEN

REECE

My best friend is sitting beside me in the Bugatti, out for a cruise to clear my mind. He's fiddling with the sunroof button, cursing under his breath.

"How's this fucking thing work?"

"It doesn't, dufus. Leave it the fuck alone."

"Someone's undies are in a knot."

I huff. "I touched Jasper," I confess, giving my best friend side eye to see his reaction. He smirks.

"Did you now?"

"Yeah, and I fucking came so hard."

"Just from a touch?"

I shake my head. And Malyk gives me an upturned smile questioning me.

"Yeah, fucked I know. His kiss was what made me come though, but his hands on me and his kiss, fuck Mal. I can't tell you how good it felt."

Malyk gives me his hyena laugh. The insane cackling that drives me insane, and taunts, "He's got your bleeding fucked up heart involved."

I turn my gaze to him, glaring at him as I respond, "Fuck no. I don't have a heart."

Malyk laughs again, so loud my car vibrates. "It might be black but it's beating inside your damn chest, and Capullo makes it beat harder."

Malyk puts his hand on my chest to feel my racing heart. It is beating erratically. I brush it off, screaming, "Get your hands off me, Mal."

"Your heart is racing sweetness," he informs me as though I can't feel my heart thumping in my chest during this conversation about Jasper. "You speak of him and your heart races."

"Doesn't mean shit," I snap back, gripping the steering wheel tightly and careening hard around the corner into Capullo territory.

Malyk reaches over, his hand on my thigh, way too close to my dick. He looks right at me, asking in a snide tone, "So you wouldn't mind if I put the moves on Jasper?"

I seethe, glaring at him even though I should be concentrating on driving.

"Touch him and I'll kill you, Mal," I seethe at him. "You know I'm a monster and could carve you seven different ways so your body is unrecognisable even to your dear uncle."

Malyk chuckles. "He's fucked you up dearest."

"No, Mal. I'm going to fuck him up. Jasper Capullo is going down."

Malyk laughs, in a scoffing snide way, taunting me, "Be careful my sweet or you'll be going down with him. You know separating sex and love is hard to do."

"I'm not going to fall for the enemy, Malyk."

"I feel you've already fallen victim, my sweet."

"You're mistaken, Mal. It's sex."

"Whatever you believe, dearest."

I slap his cheek. "Quit with the terms of endearment, fucker."

He giggles. "Say it again, Reeeeece!" he drawls out my name.

"What, weirdo?"

"Say fucker again, with that sexy rasp in your voice."

I pull up the car at the beach, cutting the engine and getting out. Malyk dances around the front of the car, following me down to the sand.

"Seriously Mal, you're an odd fucker," I tease, ensuring I hit the word 'fucker' with a raspy flick of my tone.

"Mmm, if you weren't so hung up on Capullo, I'd be on my knees worshipping you whilst you call me your fucker."

I grip his t-shirt and yank him towards me. "I hate Jasper Capullo."

Malyk gasps, smirking at me taunting, "But you love me, my fucker?"

"No, I don't know how to love."

Malyk breaks away from my hold. "Pity, love would make a man out of you, my sweet."

"Grrr," I groan, turning away from my best friend's glare to stomp towards the ocean. I flip him off and dive into waves, fully clothed. I can hear Malyk behind me chuckling as he runs into the ocean. I flip and lay on my back, floating with the sun beating down on my face. It's an attempt to block out the tension flooding my body as I relive the moments of last night with Jasper over and over in my head. It's a shame it does nothing.

CHAPTER TWELVE

Jasper

Despite my now being at university and not living at home, my father is still expecting me to keep up appearances and to attend family events and fortnightly mass. To me it's hell on earth, something that I haven't connected with in years. It's ritualistic, reciting words that have no meaning to me but I know them off by heart and robotically repeat them back at the required times.

Today I'm running late, and careen through the creaky wooden doors of the church, hoping that the whole congregation doesn't stop mid mass to stare at the latecomer. A hymn is playing so the creak isn't heard and I sneak around the back of the pews to where my parents are sitting in the second pew as always. My father gives me a death glare, shaking his head at me. I mutter, "Sorry father." His response is a scoff, and he pulls on my sleeve to force me to sit down in the pew beside him.

The mass continues and I recite the words, dreading the sermon and what the twat of a priest is going to shove down our throats with his words today. I stare absentmindedly at the crucifix on the wall. It feels like Jesus is judging me, crucifying me for what I've done with Reece. It's been drummed into me my whole life that being gay–or anything other than heterosexual–is a sin. And not just a sin but a deadly sin, one so immoral that I'm going to hell and going to burn for eternity for the things I've done. The crazy thing is though when I'm with Reece I don't feel like I'm sinning. The pleasure doesn't feel like it could be a sin, doesn't feel wrong at all.

The sermon begins, and I sink into the pew when I hear the priest mention 'Sodom and Gomorrah.' His words turn my insides, the bible verses he's reading about sulphur raining down on them for their immoral acts. With each word my self loathing increases, and I can feel my skin itching as though sulphur is covering every inch of me. I need to get out of this hell. I go to stand, but my father yanks me back down, leaning in to whisper in my ear, "You will take heed of Father Michael's words, son."

I scoff, sinking lower into the pew, hoping that a chasm will open up in the floor and swallow me whole. I'll most likely land in hell, but honestly being there is probably what I deserve for the sins I've committed so far with Reece.

The rest of the mass goes by in monotony, and I rush out of the church without even a word to my father. My skin is still crawling, and I rush back to the dorms desperate to wash away the past couple of hours. If I scrub at my skin, maybe then I'll feel clean, atoned of my sins.

Creeping into the bathroom, and towards the showers, I check each open cubicle to make sure no one is around. Thankfully, as it's late there isn't another soul in here. I like showering at this hour because it's quiet.

I put my robe and clean boxers down on the bench seat, and strip off my current clothes before turning the water on.

It's only just turned warm when I step under it, and panic hearing the door creak open. No one has come into the bathroom before at this hour. And I'm admittedly scared that I'm alone and naked with no defence. I cover myself up with my hand cupping my dick and reach out to turn off the shower but I don't get to shut it off completely as a shadowy figure comes in and steps in the shower cubicle with me. I close my eyes, my heartbeat increasing.

I'm going to die, alone and naked.

A voice booms around me, "Why are you covering up your gorgeous body when no one is here, Jasp?" My heartbeat quickens for a completely different reason, and I open my eyes as Reece leans in, kissing my neck, biting down to bruise my skin. The sensation causes goosebumps to rise on my body, and I shiver.

Gulping, but not turning around to face him, I ask, "What are you doing here, Reece?"

Reece laughs. "I'm here to make you fall to your knees for me, Capullo." Those words cause my dick to jolt. His teasing words and the way he uses my surname as a taunt never fail to turn me on. And I hate it.

"Not going to happen, Montserrat," I snap back, glancing down at my hardening dick and cursing my body for its reaction to him.

"So you say, Jasper," Reece rasps as he reaches around my body and grips my dick in his open hand, his body pressed up against my back getting his clothes wet. "But you're already hard for me and I've barely touched you."

"I was thinking about someone else," I respond, trying to sound convincing but failing as my voice is shaky.

"Liar."

"Arsehole," I bite back.

"Mmm," Reece moans, reaching down between us and cupping my arse cheeks in his hands. Involuntarily I moan, because his touch on forbidden skin feels amazing. "Don't touch me, Reece."

Reece doesn't listen, however, lowering his hands until his finger finds my hole. His other hand reaches over to grab the soap and he lathers it in his hand, sliding that finger down and slipping the tip inside me, pushing in slowly causing a moan to fall from my lips. I feel the burn of him pushing past the ring of muscle till he is knuckle deep. His finger—just one—slips in and out of my arse, and it's sending shivers of pleasure through my entire body. He slips another finger inside my hole, causing slight pain as he stretches me, scissoring them apart and hitting a spot inside me that causes me to scream out, "Oh god, Reece!"

He pulls his fingers out, sliding three inside me and hitting that spot again. The pain is all but gone, all I feel is so full. "What're you doing to me?"

"Feel good, Jasp?" he questions, his voice strained, husky and sexy. "You gonna come?"

"Yes. Oh. God. Yes. Fuck," I moan, shooting come onto the shower cubicle wall.

glare at the mess I just made, ashamed of

around, Capullo."

"No. I can't," I mumble, my cheeks heating with a blush knowing he'll see the come still dripping from my dick, even though the tiles of the shower are covered.

"Turn the fuck around," Reece demands, squeezing my butt cheeks.

I don't move so Reece shoves me forward until I'm against the wall, and he grips my waist to spin me around, soaking his body from the water still flowing from the shower head, forcefully kissing me and stealing the breath from my lungs. His kiss is punishing, bruising my lips like he bruised my neck earlier. It feels incredible. And I hate it but want more.

He withdraws his mouth from mine before I can truly kiss him back, his forehead against mine as he questions huskily, "Did you like me finger fucking your tight hole, Capullo?"

"No. I hated it. Hate you," I spit at him.

Reece chuckles, smirking. "You loved it, Jasper. Don't deny how fucked up you are my pretty boy." Those words stir my insides in a fluttery way. No one has ever called me pretty. And I don't hate it.

"I'm not yours. I'll never be yours."

"We'll see about that," Reece taunts, grabbing the cross necklace hanging around my neck. He pokes it, grabbing it in between his fingers.

"Why do you wear this ugly thing around your neck?"

"Let it go," I demand, my voice quivering.

"Why? Afraid I'll strangle you with it?"

"No, it's special to me," I tell him, shakily.

"Oh, your mummy give it to you?"

"No," I reply, sniffing back tears. "It was my grandfather's. The only one thing I have of his."

"That's pathetic you're crying over a memory, Capullo."

"Is not."

Reece flips over the necklace, and glares at the engravings before using the necklace as a means of yanking my lips to his for a kiss.

"Do you go to his grave?"

"Sometimes. On the anniversary of his death by a Montserrat."

"Oh, when's that?"

"Not telling you," I respond blushing.

"Must be soon then," Reece taunts, again kissing me hard.

I groan, pushing at Reece's chest. "Stop kissing me."

"Not a chance, Capullo. You love my kisses you dirty fucker."

"I don't. Stop putting words in my mouth and thoughts in my head."

Reece laughs. "How about I put something else in your pretty mouth?"

"No. I'm not doing that," I tell him, shaking my head.

Reece laughs again, stripping out of his clothes. I can't tear my eyes away, fixing them on him as he discards each item he's wearing.

"You've already gotten me wet, Capullo. It's the least you could do for causing me to have to leave this place naked or in your damn boxers."

He's naked now, his wet clothes on the floor of the shower and his hard dick is jutting out between us. I'm just staring, not able to take my eyes off his long hard dick, the tip peeking out already pearling with precum.

"Like what you see, Capullo?" he taunts me with what could only be described as a wicked smirk.

"Nope. Your dick is a sight," I quip, my breathing heavy as I'm lying. His dick is a sight but a beautiful one.

"Hmm, then why are you panting like a dog and glaring at it, eager to suck me off?"

"I'm not sucking your rank dick, Montserrat."

Reece chuckles and grips my neck to kiss me hard. Against my lips, he rasps, "Yes you fucking are." He breaks the kiss, staring me down. "Get on your fucking knees, Capullo."

He pushes me down to my knees. I'm annoyed that I'm not stronger to fight him off, but frankly, I don't want to. The tip of Reece's dick brushes my lips, causing a meek gasp to escape my lips.

"Suck it, Capullo," Reece demands.

I shake my head, licking my lips which causes my tongue to graze Reece's slit.

"No," I verbalise, my voice barely a whisper because quite frankly I'm not opposed to Reece's request. Reece yanks on my hair, tilting my head up. "Suck my fucking dick, Capullo."

He pulls me closer and I take his dick into my mouth, giving in and licking his length. It's insane but I actually like it, so much so that I moan around his dick.

"Yeah, fuck...feels so good, Jasp," Reece coaxes, as he starts thrusting into my mouth. It's an odd sensation, kinda like sucking on one of those long ice lollies but it's warm and velvety under my tongue.

"You're gonna make me come, Capullo."

Reece's dick hits the back of my throat, suddenly and I cough, pulling off.

"Damn, Capullo. For a prude, you can sure suck a dick. Ready for my cock to fill your mouth with come?"

"No. Fuck yourself."

He grips my hair tighter, forcing my mouth open so he can thrust his dick back into my mouth, harder and faster.

"Suck it."

I groan, obeying his demand by sucking and licking his dick until he again hits the back of my throat, his dick throbbing as he lets go of his orgasm. His come is warm and salty and I swallow it down before pulling off. Some come drips down my chin. Reece pulls me to my feet and before I can lick it away he kisses me, his tongue sweeping over my lips to lick the come away.

"Good boy, Capullo."

"Fuck you, Montserrat."

"A guy can dream, Jasp," Reece taunts, stepping out of the shower cubicle, smirking at me as he picks up my clean, dry boxers and robe and puts them on.

"Good luck getting back to your dorm room, Capullo," he jeers as he leaves.

I pick up Reece's wet clothes and throw them out of the cubicle screaming, annoyed at myself for again giving into Reece and loving it way too much.

CHAPTER THIRTEEN

Jasper

It's nearly dark as I weave through the headstones of the Capullo Vemore Cemetery. The trees are swaying in the lashing winds, casting an eeriness over the place that's foreboding even more so than being in a place that bridges heaven and hell. There are shadows lurking in the coming darkness and I'm on edge, feeling as though being here this evening is going to be unsettling.

I'm furious with myself for slipping information to Reece about coming here on the anniversary of my grandfather's death. Giving the enemy information like that was an imbecile move. I've given him something he can use against me and my family. The feud between our families—over territory and money—has been going on for generations, so far back I don't even know where, how, or when it truly began. My grandfather was the most noble man in my family, more concerned with loving his family than money.

Stepping up to his grave I sigh, picking up the dried, yellowing flowers on the base of the headstone. I cast them aside and place the fresh bunch of bright white daisies down, sitting cross legged on the grass in front.

Brushing the dust off the headstone I murmur, "Hello grandfather."

The wind whips up around me, curling the leaves and the discarded flowers up from the ground to whirl around my body. It sends a shiver through me.

"I know I've sinned grandfather," I begin, picking up one of the daisies and plucking off the petals one by one. "He is my enemy, but more. He is not at all how the world perceives him to be."

The wind whips up again, as though my grandfather is speaking to me from beyond the grave, giving me his opinion. He was always open, and accepting of me just being me. Memories collide into my mind—as I'm staring at the inscription on his headstone—of a time when I was sitting on his lap in the parlour of his—now ours—grand mansion on the highest hill in Vemore. I was showing him my latest drawing of two boys holding hands as they ran into the ocean waves. His comment was, 'Is this you, angioletto?' I'd nodded, responding with a smile and 'sì, con il mio ragazzo'. Grandfather had nodded, kissing my cheek and telling me, 'ama chi desideri'. I'd not known his meaning then, but his meaning was clearer now. I'd said 'boyfriend' meaning male partner, not boy friend in a platonic way.

The sky is darkening now, and I read the inscription again out loud, "In love we find hope, in death we find peace."

Those words hurt my heart. Grandfather only found peace in death, leaving this world the only thing that was able to get him out of the fucked up feud of the past. He'd had hope, loving my Grandmother until death parted them, and I don't doubt they're still in love in their heavenly home also. But I'm still stuck with a father who can't let go of the feud, despite his father wishing for peace for his family with his final breaths. I don't wish for death, but I wish for love and the hope it will give me. I wish that in loving who I want peace comes to my family, but I know I'm probably being delusion in thinking such things.

Now the sun is setting, the wind has died down, and I stand up to leave. The edgy feeling is back, the calm I was feeling moments ago remembering my grandfather gone.

I glance around, surveying the headstones and tall trees, shaking as I call out, "is someone there?"

An almost ghostly figure steps out from behind a tree, practically floating towards me. My head is telling me to run, but my feet appear stuck to the ground, my trepidation pinning me there.

The figure gets closer, and it's no ghost, but a combat boot wearing devil in the flesh.

"Fancy seeing you here, Jasper..." he drawls out raspy, stepping into my personal space so I stumble backwards until my butt collides with grandfather's headstone. His kiss crashes against my lips, and I groan, wanting to push him away and closer at the same time. He shouldn't be here.

CHAPTER FOURTEEN

REECE

Every damn night for the past week I'd been hanging out in the cemetery from dusk until late evening, just waiting and hoping to find Jasper visiting his grandfather's grave. I'd staked out the entire Capullo Vemore cemetery and delved into the historical records to ensure I was near the right grave. I'd followed him tonight, snuck in with the shadows and waited—whilst smoking a joint—until he was set to leave.

Stepping out from behind the tree I stalk towards him, right into his space and so close I can touch him when I taunt, "Fancy seeing you here, Jasper…"

He doesn't get a word in, as I step closer causing him to stumble back until his arse collides with the headstone. He still doesn't get to respond with words, as I crash my lips to his, stealing his breath. He groans into the kiss, his hands come up to cup my jaw and pull me closer.

I chuckle against his lips, breaking the kiss. "Eager to see me huh, Capullo?"

"Never. You cornered me."

"Did I now?"

"Yes, you shouldn't be here Reece."

"Yeah, probably," I respond laughing. "What are you going to do about it? Call the cops on me?"

He shakes his head. "I didn't bring my phone. Such earthly possessions should not be brought into a sacred place."

I scoff. "Pftt, Jasp, you sound like a damn lunatic sometimes."

"I'm not anything of the sort! The only lunatic here right now is you."

I grip his neck, squeezing it hard enough to cause him to gasp. "Such horrid words, Capullo. Here I was thinking you were a sweet, shy bible boy."

"I...I...don't..."

"What are you trying to say, Jasp?"

"Nothing," he pants, and I rip my hand away, sliding it down his torso to cup his dick in my palm. "I don't want you here."

I squeeze his dick a little, and a hiss escapes his lips before he bites down on his lower lip to the point of it bleeding.

"You say that as though you want me to care about what you want," I taunt him, before kissing him again, harder and with enough force to bruise his plump lips. He groans, thrusting his hips forward so his growing erection fills my hand. I rub it slowly, kissing him harder and licking across his lips to taste the blood leaking from the mark he'd made.

His hands again seek my body out, this time he threads them around my waist and yanks my body closer so my dick brushes against my hand stroking him. He breaks the kiss with a loud moan.

"More. Reece...more...please..." he begs, his voice cracking.

"More? You want more?"

"Yes..." he rasps. "Please touch me, make me come."

"You ask for too much, my pretty boy."

"Don't call me that!" he roars at me.

"I'll call you whatever I wish, Capullo," I taunt him, reaching around to grip his arse and slapping it. "And you'll do what I ask like the good boy you are."

"I'm not a good boy," he snaps, his eyes darkening as his pupils go wide.

"Yeah, you think you're a bad boy huh?"

He nods, stammering, "Yes. I'm a sinner. A bad boy."

"Mmm, my bad boy, my pretty boy," I taunt, kissing him. He moans against my mouth, grinding against me, causing my dick to harden in my jeans.

Only just parting our lips, I utter softly, "Turn around and hold onto the headstone, pretty boy."

He glares at me, a question on the tip of his tongue that he doesn't verbalise as he turns his body around, grabbing the top of the headstone in clenched hands.

He turns his head back to stare at me, waiting for my next taunt.

I step up behind him, gripping the waistband of his sweats and tugging them down. He's wearing the ugliest underwear on the planet, tight plain cotton black undies, covered in stains. I thought the fucker was rich, but these undies scream poverty.

"What's with the jocks?"

"They're my favourite. So comfy," he moans.

"Well, they're ugly as fuck, Jasp," I tell him. "So I'm sure you won't mind if I rip them."

He gasps but doesn't make a move to stop me as I grip the leg elastic of the jocks, yanking each side apart until they rip straight down the middle exposing his arse cheeks.

"Reece!" he yells at me, giving me an angry glare.

"Whoops," I snicker, sliding a finger in between the ripped cotton to seek out his pucker.

I find it easily, and tease it, rubbing my finger over his flesh. He bucks his hips back.

"Mmm, please…" he begs, not tearing his gaze away from mine.

"Please? That all you can say, Capullo?"

He doesn't respond so I taunt him more, "Tell me what you want, Jasper. Tell me what you want me to do to you."

I push the tip of my finger against his pucker and he moans, "That. Touch me there. That spot."

"It'll hurt if I do that, Capullo," I tell him, pushing my finger in a little more.

"I know," he responds. "But as a sinner, I deserve the hurt."

His words cause my heart to quicken. I honestly don't want to hurt him. I'm not a sadist when it comes to sex.

"Fuck, Jasper," I groan, yanking the jocks down to his ankles, and gripping the top of his Converse high tops to spread his legs wider.

Crouching down I grip his arse cheeks, spreading him wider so I can see his puckered hole.

"Damn, Capullo," I groan, kissing his pucker.

"Fuck!" he roars, bucking back against my face as I place another kiss against his pulsing ring of muscle.

"More, Reece, more…do that again."

I laugh, slipping my tongue inside his hole, and darting it in and out. His tight hole pulses under my tongue and he arches his back to push my tongue deeper inside him.

Reaching up, I slide a finger inside him, curling it upwards to caress his prostate whilst still laving my tongue over his pucker.

"Fuck!, Reece! Please don't stop," he calls out, his hips starting to shake as his release builds.

I withdraw my finger and stop licking to stand. Jasper groans, giving me a death glare. "Can't have you coming yet, Capullo."

"You're an arsehole, Montserrat."

I want to say something snide in response, about my just having my finger and tongue in his arsehole but I refrain, instead I stare at his perky arse still jutted out towards me as I unbutton my jeans and shove them and my boxers down to my ankles.

I tug on his hair, yanking him back against my chest. "Open your legs, pretty boy."

He grunts, "Can't."

"Just fucking do it, Capullo, or I'll rip your sweats in two as well."

He stretches his legs apart more, the sound of the fabric of his sweats tearing apart makes a whimper escape his lips.

CAZ MAY

I take his cut jaw in my grip and tip his head back for a kiss. "Sorry, not sorry pretty boy."

"Arsehole," he spits at him.

"Haha, you love me, Jasp," I tease.

"No, I hate you."

"Yeah, mutual pretty boy, but you love being dirty for me," I taunt him, bumping my pelvis against his back, my dick slipping between his thighs. The tip of my dick only just pokes out under his, and I slowly start thrusting, each back and forth grazing along his balls and taint.

"Oh god, fuck, Reece," he calls out, biting down on his lips to hold in his moans. I kiss him, still thrusting him and increasing the pace as I fuck his mouth with my tongue, biting down on his lips to draw blood.

Against his puffy, red, kiss swollen lips, I taunt, "Don't you ever hide your moans, pretty boy."

I reach down and grab his dick in my fist, stroking him in time with fucking his thighs.

"More, Reece, please make me come," he begs. I tease his slit with my fingertip, using his precum as lube, stroking him harder.

"You wanna come, pretty boy?"

"Yes, yes, Reece!" he responds huskily, pushing back so my dick slides down his and I'm able to grab both of our dicks in my hand and stroke us together.

"Am I the only one who can make you come, Capullo?"

"Yes! Reece!," he bellows, letting go and spilling ropes of come all over the headstone. He's trembling, riding out his release as I follow, my dick jerking up and covering his with my come. Stepping back I shove him away.

And he turns around, stumbling on the pile of clothes at his feet. He's whimpering, tears stinging his eyes. My heart thumps in my chest. That felt so fucking good, and I know he enjoyed it as much as I did, so why the fucker is crying is beyond me. I watch him pull up his ripped undies and sweats, laughing as I do the same. I'm fucked.

CHAPTER FIFTEEN

Jasper

Letting out a whimper as Reece lets me go, I sniff back the tears stinging my eyes. Reece is laughing as I pull up his ripped clothing, upset that it barely covers my body, and upset that Reece is being so callous.

I'm appalled with myself for letting Reece do that—causing me to sin—in a sacred place. And I'm appalled with myself for giving into Reece again, for letting him use my body in a salacious way. It felt incredible, so pleasurable but it was a great sin.

I run off, leaving Reece at the gravesite laughing. My feet pound the pavement, leading me straight to the door of the only person I can speak to about such things.

She opens the door almost immediately upon my knock and seeing me on her doorstep, crying she gapes in shock, asking, "Jasp, what happened?"

I step across the threshold, follow her to the bedroom and sit down on the bed next to her. She doesn't say anything, just rubs a hand up my bare arm.

"Nanc," I sob, sniffing back the tears again, and wiping my arm over my face. "I…I hate myself," I stammer, glancing down at my crotch and the ripped seam of my sweats.

"Why?" she questions me, her voice soft but probing.

"Because of Reece," I admit, adding in a lower tone, "And what I let him do to me."

"What did you do this time?" she asks, this time her voice has a teasing girly tone.

"I can't verbalise my sins to you, Nancy. They're too sordid to admit to doing."

"But Jasp, hiding from your sins will only hurt your mind." Her words are so wise, as usual with Nancy. However, today they annoy me.

"Don't patronise me, Nancy," I snap at her, balling my fists in frustration. I feel like screaming. "I know I've done wrong, but yet I can't seem to stop thinking about him, and the acts of indecency we've committed together."

"How indecent?" she enquires, raising her eyebrow at me.

I sigh, admitting, "Naked trysts involving our hands and mouths on our penises until orgasms, Nanc."

Nancy gasps and then laughs softly. "Firstly Jasp, please use the word dick and secondly say come, and thirdly, damn you dirty boy." Her tone is teasing, causing me to blush.

"I have been dirty, and I feel so tarnished but it feels so pleasurable in the moment," I comment, thinking back to the feel of Reece's fingers and tongue inside me, his kiss on my lips.

"Sexual acts are meant to be pleasurable, Jasp," Nancy responds, nodding to affirm her words.

"Yes, but should be saved for the sanctity of marriage," I remark.

Nancy scoffs and goes to reply, but I don't let her respond, blurting out, "I hate him. I hate that he defiles me."

"Do you really, Jasper? Or do you just hate that being with the one person you're born to hate is the only thing that feels right?"

I exhale, once more sniffing back tears stinging my eyes. "That. I hate that," I comment with a huff.

Nancy reaches out, pulling me into a hug. Her delicate hands stroke my hair.

"I know Jasp," she soothes as I cry into her shoulder, thinking about Reece, how he makes me feel bewildered by pleasure I didn't know was possible. And at the same time, I'm contemplating Nancy's words about being with him feeling right even though it's wrong. I hate Reece Montserrat, despite the fact that he makes me feel alive and desiring more of his wickedness.

CHAPTER SIXTEEN

REECE

Doing Dad's bidding—his murders of those who've double crossed or threatened him—sucks donkey dick. I'd only come 'home' from the dorms to grab some clothes and the food I'd had stashed in my cupboard for Raven. I was just about to leave, my hand on the doorknob when I heard his bellowing voice, "Reece! Get in here now, boy!"

He's roaring from his office, the door not even open but his voice is that damn loud it can be heard through solid wood.

Gripping the handle tighter I consider leaving, and ignoring him, however, he'll be blowing up my phone in seconds and probably deny me the money for the job he wants me to do for being a brat.

He bellows again, "Reece Mattheus Montserrat!!"

Eh, the full name card.

I cross the grand hallway, stepping up to his office doors and swinging them open with a shove of my shoulder.

He inspects me as I enter the room. "You called for me, father?" I question in an angelic tone. I don't speak to anyone the way I do to him. If he heard the way I spoke to everyone else in my life he'd probably spank me with his belt.

"Yes, I have a job for you. A rather ghastly one."

I scoff. "Your jobs are always ghastly father."

He shakes his head, standing and gripping the edge of his mahogany desk, reading something on the papers in front of him.

"This one requires you to be discreet and ruthless."

"Seriously? What kinda fucked up thing have you got yourself involved in now?" I question, immediately regretting my words when he stomps towards me seething.

He grips my collar, yanking me closer and practically spitting in my face with his enraged voice, "You will not question my engagements nor speak to me with such insolence, boy!"

I shove a hand against his chest. "Fuck you, father!"

He's seething again, his throat and face blood red.

"Don't test me, Reece."

"Wasn't doing anything of the sort," I remark. "I'm just over doing your bidding."

"Well, son," he says in a patronising tone, "you know what the consequences of not doing your job would be. No trust fund, no car, and you can kiss university goodbye."

I shrug, staring him down.

"You going to do the job?" he finally asks when I don't respond to his threats.

"If I must."

"Good. You're to go to the Cassidy Club, and find a man by the name of Ron Roberts."

I nod. "What's this fucker done?"

"He assaulted our best girl, and violated the club consent terms."

"So what am I doing about it?"

"What must be done, Reece. Make him regret the day he stepped into a Montserrat premises."

Again I nod, feeling giddy about getting to fuck up a filthy man. I'm about to head out the door when I ask, "What girl are we talking about?"

Dad shakes his head, scoffing, and sitting back down in his foreboding leather desk chair. I mumble, "Fine don't tell me then. Just thought I should know whose virtue I'm defending.

I open the door, stepping out in the hallway when I hear Dad respond softly, under his breath, "It was Katee."

And there it is. Katee Martinez may as well be his daughter. They're oddly close, and he'd do anything to protect her. At one point he'd even made an offer to pay her a wage without her having to work at the club, but she refused. Apparently, she enjoys dancing in skimpy outfits and offering lap dances for extra cash.

From by the door, I grab my gym bag, and head out to the Bugatti, shoving it on the front seat beside me before I speed off towards the club.

Sliding the Bugatti into a car spot right out the front of the club, I flick the lock and stomp inside. Dad had said to be discreet with this kill, but noticing Bartholomew manning the counter I know that's not necessary. My cousin knows what I'm forced to do. And he's no blabbermouth either.

Stepping up to the counter, I greet him, "Barth, my cuz, how's it hanging?"

He holds up his hand, clasping mine in our usual slapping handshake. "Reece, my cuz. It's hanging low. Shit's been happening around here."

"So I've heard."

He leans forward, saying into my ear, "You hear about Katee?"

"Yeah, getting that fucker is why I'm here," I mumble, touching my waistband to make sure my gun is tucked in tight.

Barth nods. "He's right over near the stage. Dickwad with the red mohawk."

I glance towards the stage where Summer is dancing. The dickhead in question is staring right at her, salivating.

"Thanks, cuz. Got the keys for a private room for me?"

He gives me a wink, telling me, "No need for keys, cuz. I've unlocked the private room at the back for you. And left a few goodies for you to play with."

My heart races in anticipation. Seems some torture is on the cards tonight. You don't cross a Montserrat or someone we care about without facing dire consequences. And in Ron Roberts case those consequences are torturous, and his death will be his reprieve.

"Thanks cuz, looking forward to playing with his sorry arse."

"Anytime cuz, go make that fucker pay for hurting our Katee." He frowns.

"You told her yet?"

He shakes his head. "No."

"You need to, Barth. Katee loves you, and I know it's hurting you both hanging around this toxic hellhole."

"Yeah, but I'm shit scared of putting my heart on the line and telling her I love her. It's good with us, and I don't want words to fuck up what we have."

"Yeah, I get it cuz. But Katee's your endgame."

"I know. I'd fucking die protecting her."

"Tell her cuz."

"I will. After you take down the fucker who hurt her."

I nod, chuckling as I stalk across the club towards my prey.

Stepping up behind him–just as Summer's set is ending and the room is silent for a beat–I lean in and murmur in his ear, "Hi gorgeous, love the mohawk."

He gasps, stumbling backwards, and then turning to face me. He eyes my body and then scoffs. "I don't fuck guys."

I laugh in response. "Wasn't asking for a fuck."

"Then why are you soliciting with compliments?"

"Can't a guy compliment another on a sick hairstyle?"

"Not if he's straight."

"You homophobic, Rob?"

He gasps, his mouth agape. I push it closed with my finger, laughing.

"How do you know my name?" he stammers, stumbling on his feet to get away from me.

I stalk closer, gripping his arm. "I know a lot about you, Rob."

"Yeah, like what?"

"That you're a regular here at my father's club, and that you're not a respectful patron."

His eyes boggle, and he shakes his head, mumbling, "No. No. No. Fucking way."

"You've heard of me?"

"Yeah, and I...I know you're a fag."

"Guilty, but at least I'm not a pathetic man like you."

"I didn't do anything to her that she didn't ask for."

"Oh, so you admit to being with our girl?"

"What, no, I mean..."

I chuckle. "Come with me, Rob."

He opens his mouth to say something but only an 'eek' comes out, a squeak of sorts. I grab his arm and drag him away. He's weak as fuck, not even fighting back as I drag him to the private rooms at the back of the club.

The back one is unlocked and opening the door I shove him inside. He falls to the ground, shrinking away from me. I lock the door behind me and take a moment to admire the 'toys' Barth has left for me. A small sledgehammer, an icepick, some pliers, fishing lures and a large serrated knife.

I pick up the knife, running my finger down the non-serrated side. "These look like fun."

Rob is still on the floor, clutching his knees to his chest whilst whimpering.

He spits at me as I approach him, taunting him with the knife pointed at him.

"Tell me what you did to Katee?"

"Nothing. I didn't touch her!"

"That's not what I heard," I tell him, pressing the serrated edge of the knife against his forehead.

He whimpers again. "Don't hurt me, please," he begs.

"You gonna talk? Tell me what you did."

"I told you, nothing. It was just a lap dance like all clubgoers are entitled to."

"If it was just a lap dance I wouldn't be here fucker."

I take a step back, putting the knife back on the table and grabbing the pliers. I stand over his legs then, gripping his hair in a fist to tilt his head back.

"What...are...you...doing?" he stammers his voice raspy breaths.

"Making you talk, and thinking about yanking your teeth out one by one."

He yelps as I yank on his hair more for his mouth to open. His eyes are glassy as though he's about to cry, and I let out a callous laugh pushing the closed pliers between his lips.

He tries to speak, but he doesn't have a chance as I pry the pliers open, stretching open his mouth. The tip of the pliers close around his very front tooth, and I wrench the pliers out of his mouth taking the tooth with them. He lets out a deafening scream.

And I laugh maniacally, asking him, "Gonna talk now?"

"Seriously, what kinda psycho are you?"

"Your worst nightmare, if you don't talk."

"Fine, I touched her," he yells at me. "Happy?"

"Did she consent to that?"

He scoffs. "No. She's a fucking stripper, and she was grinding on my lap."

"So that gives you the right to touch her?"

He laughs and spits out the blood filling his mouth right at me.

"Yeah, the bitch got me hard."

I stare at him, contemplating my next move. I can tell he's not telling me everything. He did more than touch her.

I put the pliers down and pick up the sledgehammer. His eyes boggle.

"And what did you do next? Where'd you touch her? Did you kiss her?"

"What do you think fag?"

"I think you're a coward and a liar."

"I'm telling you I touched her. That's all."

"So your tiny dick was hard and you did nothing but touch her?"

He nods, but can't look me in the eyes.

I step closer to him again, grabbing his thighs and yanking his legs down, spreading them wide to stand in between them.

I bend down so I'm at eye level with him. "Liar," I spit at him.

"I'm...I'm...telling no lies."

"You know what I do to liars?"

He shakes his head but makes no response.

"I fuck them up until they admit what they did or they can't."

Again he makes no move to say anything, but he's shivering with his eyes focusing on the sledgehammer.

"You gonna speak or what?"

"I'm not telling you anything."

"Your choice, fucker," I taunt, holding the sledgehammer up a moment before bringing it down forcefully onto his crotch. He squeals, cursing out, "FUCK!!" as he clutches his balls.

"You fucking psycho! Why'd you do that?"

"So you'll never get hard again. I know you fucked her."

"Fine, if I tell you the truth will you let me go?"

"I guess you'll find out," I taunt.

Still clutching his crotch he sighs and then says, "I ripped off her clothes and touched every inch of her hot as fuck body."

I'm staring him down, listening to every word whilst cringing inside. I don't think Barth knows exactly what happened to his girl and once I've offed this fucker I'm going mute. Bartholomew only needs to know that his girl needs time and his love.

"And then I fucked her until she was begging me."

"Begging you to stop?"

"I don't fucking know. I didn't give a shit."

There are no words to say to this piece of shit. I put the sledgehammer down, and withdraw my gun, putting it against his chest.

"Stand up," I demand. He glares at me, shaking as he stands up.

"Please...don't," he begs. "I...told...you the truth."

"Is that what she said while you fucked her?"

"No...she was begging for it."

"Liar," I seethe, taunting him with the gun cocked.

He spits at me again, spattering my clothes with blood. I'd only pulled out one tooth, so it's baffling that his mouth is filled with so much blood.

"Strip, fucker," I demand. He shakes his head.

I press the gun against his forehead. "Strip, you fucker."

He obeys, slowly until he's completely naked in front of me.

"Are you going to fuck me now? To punish me?"

I scoff. "You'd like that too much for it to be a punishment."

"What are you going to do to me then?" he asks, his voice shaky.

"What you deserve…" I tell him, smirking wickedly as I pull the gun away from his head and take a step back. The gun has six bullets in it, and I plan on using every damn one of them.

"What's th…" he starts to ask but I fire a round, the bullet hurtling towards him and cutting off his words. It hits the target, spattering blood everywhere as it collides with his dick and he screams the soundproof room down.

I don't even flinch as I fire another two rounds, this time the bullets hit him square in the ribcage, spattering even more blood. He's screaming in agony.

"Pll…eese…stt…ooop…" he yelps.

I'm shocked he's even still standing, let alone trying to speak. "Too late," I spit, stepping towards him and firing a bullet into each kneecap. He falls to the floor, blood spurting out of every bullet wound.

I put the gun to his head, and he lets out a final gasp for breath, a final plea to beg me to stop but it's worthless. I draw back the trigger and fire the final shot straight between his eyes. The blood spatter covers me, and he falls backwards into a pool of his own blood. I kick his lifeless body just for fun and tuck my gun back into the waistband of my jeans.

I could've tortured him more, but the job is done.

Heading back out to the desk, I stop to speak to Barth.

"It's done. You good to organise disposal?"

"Yeah, cuz. Thanks."

"Anytime for you, Barth. Don't forget to comfort your girl after this."

"I will."

"I won't tell you all the details, but she's lucky to have you loving her."

He nods, and I leave, getting in the Bugatti and driving straight over the bridge to the side of Vemore I shouldn't be. I shouldn't even be thinking about him, let alone driving to his dorms in the middle of the night, covered in some useless fucker's blood. But I need to get out of my own head for a while, and just enjoy some pleasure that's not sadistic.

CHAPTER SEVENTEEN

Jasper

It's a warm evening so I have my window open to let in the slight breeze and I'm sitting on my bed in only boxers whilst I'm reading. It's a textbook, so it's a bit of a bore, but the artwork is stunning.

Flipping the pages I sigh, about to close it and get under the covers to try and sleep when my open window slides up. I shriek, reaching out to shut the window which isn't possible as Reece is climbing into my room again.

He's shivering, despite the warm evening.

"Reece, seriously what are you doing crawling in my window again?"

"I had to see you."

He slides over to the end of the bed and stands up. It's then I take in his outfit, black ripped at the knees jeans with a white t-shirt that's covered in blood.

He's smirking at me, and I'm aghast. His t-shirt and all up his arms are covered in blood. Blood.

He doesn't appear to be bleeding but I still ask, "Is that blood? Are you bleeding and about to die in front of me?"

Reece laughs. "I'm not bleeding," Reece assures me, stepping across my room so he's standing in front of me, his abs right in my face. "Want to lick it off?" he teases. I nearly choke on my saliva as I swallow.

"Who's blood is it?"

Reece responds, "Some random fucker I just offed for dad." His tone is low as though he's hiding something from me, not telling me the truth about what he just did. I shake my head at him. I'm getting the feeling that Reece came here–to see me–after killing someone tonight for a reason.

"Why do you do it? Kill people for him?"

He gives me a look I can't decipher. A look that makes me feel like I'm a daft fool. "Because I have to," he tells me, sitting down on the bed with one leg bent, and the other hanging over the edge. I cringe. He's sitting on my bed with blood all over him.

"I don't understand," I respond, giving him a confused glare.

"He pays my way and if I don't do his bidding, I'll kiss my trust fund away."

"So you kill people for money?"

CAZ MAY

Reece laughs, in a manically way that causes my stomach to roll with nausea.

"And for the fun of it, the thrill," he admits, pulling up the hem of his t-shirt and putting a gun on the sheets in between us. The barrel is long and slim and it's brass in colour with an intricate pattern on it, with an ornate 'M' for Montserrat I'm presuming. I don't really want to know anything else but still, I'm asking, "is that the gun you used?"

"Yeah, as well as some other things. I tortured the fucker until he confessed his depravity."

I gape at him. Torture. He tortured a man and murdered him. "And you liked doing that? Thought it was fun?"

"It was a thrill. Offing a worthless piece of shit who didn't deserve to live." His expression is blank.

"You're a psycho Reece."

He laughs then, smirking and winking at me, taunting, "But I'm your psycho right?" I scoff, about to respond when Reece kisses me, taking my breath away, and any other words I wanted to say.

I should push him away, break the kiss and tell him to get out, but I do the opposite. I kiss him deeper, grabbing the front of his t-shirt and pulling him closer so we fall back onto the bed, Reece now on top of me. He moans into my mouth, biting down on my lip to draw blood which he licks away as usual. I can feel my dick hardening between us, and I curse myself for that as I break the kiss.

"You can't keep coming here and kissing me like that," I rage at him.

He laughs, smirking in that wicked way. "Your body isn't complaining, Jasp."

"I told you, and I'll tell you again, my body is a traitor."

"Admit it, Jasper, you're attracted to me," Reece taunts, reaching down between us to slide his hand into my boxers. My hips jerk up.

"Stop, Ree..." I moan, not even able to get his full name out as he starts to stroke my hardening dick.

"Damn it, Jasp," he curses. "You really want me to stop?"

I shake my head slightly, bucking my hips up more to increase the friction. "No..." I rasp, reaching up to wrap my hands around his neck and bring his lips back down to mine.

CHAPTER EIGHTEEN

REECE

*J*asper is a contradiction. He pushes me away, says to stop touching or kissing him, and then I question him, ask if he wants me to stop, and his response is 'no'. He's kissing me now like he's starving, like he can't get enough of me, and the feeling is fucking mutual. But after tonight I'm craving more. I'm still on edge, high on the adrenaline of the kill.

I break the kiss with a groan, withdrawing my hand from Jasper's boxers and yanking my t-shirt over my head. He whimpers, pouting at me. It's cute, and fucking sexy.

I laugh. "If you want more, Jasp, take off your boxers."

He doesn't respond, just eagerly shoves his boxers down to his ankles and kicks them off. I stand from the bed, and unbutton my jeans, shoving them down and tugging them over my boots. Jasper glares at me, looking my body up and down.

"You have so many tattoos," he remarks, reaching out to touch them with his fingertips.

I don't know what to say, so I just continue undressing by wrestling off my boots. I put my knife on the bed next to my gun. Jasper just watches my every move, his eyes wide. Lastly, I push my boxers to the floor and dive back onto the bed to kiss him again.

He's writhing underneath me, our dicks colliding as they harden. I can feel the cold metal of my gun against my thigh and breaking the kiss I shift back to a sitting position on the bed and pick up my gun. Caressing it, I stare at Jasper.

He's biting on his lip again, staring back at me with that wide-eyed look again.

"I killed a man with this gun tonight," I murmur.

Jasper doesn't respond.

"You have nothing to say about that, Capullo?" I question him, leaning forward–still holding my gun in one hand–whilst I grip his dick with the other.

He gasps, biting his lip again to drive me insane. He sighs, a deep sigh as though he hasn't taken a breath for several minutes.

CAZ MAY

"Your sins are not for me to judge," he tells me, his expression and his voice not wavering. "What you choose to do with a weapon is a choice."

"Cut the biblical crap, Capullo," I snap at him, toying with the trigger of the gun for a moment. His eyes go wide again.

And my mind goes south, straight into the gutter. I click the safety on.

"What're you thinking, Reece?" he questions me, his voice meek and worried.

"Turn over, get on all fours, Jasper."

"Why? What're you going to do to me?"

"You'll find out if you are a good boy, Jasp."

He obeys my request which turns me on so much. I'm tempted to go all the way with him, to fuck him from behind, but he needs some prep before I'm fucking him. And what I'm about to do is probably cruel, but in the absence of a toy, one has to improvise.

Jasper is now on all fours, jutting his arse out towards me. I grip his cheeks and spread him open.

"So pretty, Capullo," I tease, pressing the tip of the gun barrel against his pucker.

"Oh shit...wh..." he gasps, turning back to look at me, as I press it in a little more.

"Reece..." he moans. "What are you doing to me?"

"You trust me?"

"I…ah…no…maybe…" he stammers, arching his back a little.

"Good boy," I praise, putting the gun down on the bed and picking up my knife. I slice across my index finger, pressing it with my thumb to draw some blood before I rub it all over Jasper's pucker.

He moans and hisses as I slip my finger in breaching the ring of muscle.

"Reece," he drawls, pushing his arse back to fuck my fingers when I slide a second one in. "Feels so good."

"Mmm, your hole looks so stunning with my blood all over it, pretty boy."

He gasps, looking back at me again as he questions, "Blood? Your blood?"

"Yes, Capullo, I'm marking you with my blood."

"I…ah…more," he moans in an almost incoherent tone. I withdraw my fingers and lean down to kiss his pucker, laving my tongue over the ring of muscle, licking the blood away and lubing him up more.

"Fuck, that feels good," Jasper moans, trying to fuck my tongue by pushing back. Again I pull back, causing him to let out an angry huff. I laugh and taunt him, "Just wait, pretty boy."

Once more I pick up the gun, positioning it against his pucker again. He hisses at the contact, moaning as I breach the ring of muscle with the barrel.

"Fuck, Reece!" he roars, pushing back against the trigger of the gun, drawing it in more.

"Take it, Jasper. Take it all into that tight, pretty hole."

Steadily I pull the gun out, before slamming it back inside his hole harder.

"Ohmygod, ohshit," he mumbles, glancing back at me, his eyes dark with pleasure.

"You like being fucked with my gun, Capullo?" I question, titling the barrel upwards inside him to touch his prostrate with the muzzle.

"Yes, there, oh god there!" he shouts, again rocking his hips back and forth to fuck the gun.

"That's it, pretty boy, scream the dorms down."

"Please Reece, more, I'm going to come," he rasps, once more glancing back at me. His eyes are glassy. Holding the gun inside him still, I pick up my knife in my other hand and slap the flat edge across his arse cheek.

"Ohhhhh!" he shrieks. His arse is now marked, red with a slight scratch. I withdraw the gun from his hole and bend over to lick his arse cheeks, a hint of blood swirling on my tongue.

"Reece…" he moans my name, and I clasp his hair to yank him back so his back collides with my chest.

"Kiss me, pretty boy," I rasp against his lips.

He shakes his head, a raspy, "No," escaping his lips.

"I said, kiss me, Capullo."

He moans, and I grasp his neck, slamming my lips to his and taking his tongue with mine as the moment our lips make contact he opens up for me. He defies me, but he can't help but give in.

Gasping he breaks the kiss, and moans, "Need to come."

I shove his body back down until he's flat on his stomach on the bed and spreading his legs wide I spit on his pucker, before picking up the gun again. With the muzzle against his pucker, I lube him up before shoving the barrel inside his hole again.

"Fuck the gun, Jasper," I instruct.

He does as I request without protest, his pelvis rising up and down off the bed taking the gun in and out.

"Oh, oh, fuck," he moans, fucking the sheets of his bed, getting himself off with my gun in his arse.

"Such a pretty sight, Capullo."

"Mmm, I'm…oh…shit!" he calls out, peering back at me as he comes, his whole body trembling.

Again I withdraw the gun, throwing it on the floor and he sighs, sinking into the bed. I lie down beside him, kissing his sweaty forehead.

"Good boy, Capullo."

CAZ MAY

"Don't call me that," he snaps at me, giving me a death stare as he rolls over to face me.

I chuckle, kissing him. "What do you want me to call you after sex?"

"That wasn't sex, Reece," he remarks, scoffing at me.

"Call it whatever, but I just fucked your sexy arse with a gun," I jeer, grabbing his arse cheeks in my hands, squeezing them to pull him closer to kiss him. He makes no protest of having my lips on his, but he doesn't deepen the kiss. "And you loved it. You're a dirty boy, Capullo."

"Am not," he protests, reaching down to grab my dick in his fist.

"Face it, Capullo. You're as fucked up as me, and one day soon I'm going to fuck you with my cock inside your arse so hard I'll be sending you to hell."

He stares at me wide eyed. "Don't speak so cruelly, and throw my sin back at me. My place in hell is already laid out without you violating me so."

His religious views are archaic, but he shows great conviction which I admire. He's a contradiction for sure, and fuck me dead, I'm feeling something for the guy I shouldn't be. He's messing with my feelings, my damn heart and that can't fucking happen. He's the enemy. But being with him feels so good, so right.

Glancing down I realise he's still clutching my dick. "You mind?"

"Mind what?" he asks, eyeing me with a raised eyebrow and smirk.

"Doing something useful with that hand."

He laughs and slowly starts to stroke my dick, which hardens under the touch of his long, delicate artist's hand.

CHAPTER NINETEEN

Jasper

Gripping Reece's dick tighter I stroke his length. He hardens as my fingers brush up and down his velvety skin.

"Yeah, like that, Jasp," he encourages, his hand slipping between my fingers. I dip a finger–from my other hand–into the precum leaking from his tip. He eyes me–his eyes dark with lust–when I slip it into my mouth and moan at the taste.

"Fuck, pretty boy," he curses out, jerking his dick in my hand. "I want to fuck your mouth."

I yank my hand away from his dick, stammering, "I…um…ok."

He pushes me down on the bed and straddles my body, edging up my torso until he's sitting over my ribcage and the tip of his dick is at my lips. I lick the tip, swirling my tongue in his slit, causing him to moan lasciviously.

Jerking forward he pushes his dick into my mouth, forcing me to open wide to take him in. And he starts to thrust his dick in and out, his hands then pressing against my chest, teasing my nipples to attention. And fuck it feels good. So good it sends jolts of pleasure to my dick.

His dick hits the back of my throat and I gag, forcing him to pull out.

"Damn, you take my dick down your throat so well, pretty boy."

"Ah, yeah, I…" I stammer, feeling my cheeks heat.

"What, pretty boy?" he asks, brushing his fingers over my nipples again.

"That, you teasing my nipples…I…" he cuts my words off, pinching my nipples between his fingers again causing me to moan, "Oh god! Fucker!"

"You like that, Capullo?" Reece taunts, doing it again, and sending that same pulse of pleasure to my dick.

"Yes!"

"Fuck, Jasper, you turn me on," Reece responds, still teasing my nipples as he shoves his dick back into my mouth, forcing me to suck him.

I take his dick in and out, sucking and licking, and moaning around his girth. He pulls out all the way again, and I yank him down for a kiss, murmuring against his lips, "Keep touching my nipples, and I'm going to come."

He kisses me again, teasing my nipples between his fingers for a moment. I break the kiss with a gasp, jerking my hips up and coming without him touching me. I hate him. Hate that he can bring forth pleasure of the most illicit kind in me with barely a touch.

"You're so fucking sexy, Capullo," he taunts, shoving his dick back into my open mouth. He thrusts in and out, fucking my mouth, and I lap at his skin, swirling my tongue over his flesh, until he calls out, "I'm going to fucking come!"

I nod, grabbing his balls and fondling them as he thrusts into my mouth one last time, hitting my uvula. I gag, as his release hits, his dick throbbing as his hot come spills in my mouth. "Don't you dare fucking swallow, Capullo."

My eyes go wide, and he pulls out, immediately kissing me before I can even respond. I still have his come in my mouth, and he slips his tongue between my lips to lap it up. He swirls his tongue with mine, his come covering our lips as we kiss.

"Fuck, Jasper," he moans, breaking the kiss and swallowing the come in his mouth. "Open your mouth, and show me the come, pretty boy."

Gargling I open wide and he groans. "Such a good boy for me, Capullo," he taunts, giving me another kiss. He moans, pulling back from the kiss and then murmurs, "Swallow, pretty boy."

Gulping, I swallow down the remaining come in my mouth, and Reece gives me another kiss.

"You are definitely a sexy, dirty fucker, Jasper."

"I…um…only with you, Reece," I reply, blushing at my admittance.

"It fucking better be with only me, Capullo. You're mine."

I don't respond to that, but it causes my heart to race as Reece slides back down my body to kneel at my ankles.

"You made a damn mess of yourself, Jasp."

I sit up and look at my come stained sheets. "It's your fault for making me come so much," I jeer.

"Yeah, well I do love making you come, Jasper."

"Hmm, yeah," I murmur, yawning and falling backwards.

Reece lies down next to me, giving me a deep, passionate kiss that has us both pressing our bodies against each other, tangling our legs together, our dicks brushing against each other.

Being with Reece feels so good, not like a sin at all. And honestly, if it is a sin, I'm close to not caring anymore. The pleasure I feel with Reece is blinding, even with the pain of my throbbing arse from being fucked with his gun I'm on cloud nine, and my racing heart tells me I'm falling for him. I'm falling for the enemy, the devil himself personified.

CHAPTER TWENTY

Jasper

Waking up from the best sleep I've had in weeks, I'm sore. My arse is throbbing and thoughts of last night crash into my mind, of Reece fucking me–violating me–with his gun. Rolling over I expect to find him still next to me, but Reece is gone.

I'm angry at him for skipping out sometime during the night after that. Stupid me thought something had changed between us, that he actually cared.

Stumbling out of bed I tug on a pair of lacy undies, rubbing them against my dick for a moment to feel the slight scratch on my skin. It sends a shiver through me, and I think about getting myself off by rubbing my dick with them on. But instead, I decide to confront Reece.

I dress quickly and go out to my Aston Martin to drive to the other side of Vemore. It scares me being on his side–the rough side–of town. I'm on edge, gripping the steering wheel tightly as I'm driving around, my eyes boggling at the sheer depravity of what I'm witnessing happening on the streets of the Montserrat side of Vemore.

Getting to his university I park the car and slide out. It's stupid, but I ask around for Reece. A pretty girl tells me his exact room number, which causes a pang of jealousy to hit me. I shouldn't be feeling jealous. It's a sin—most definitely one of the seven deadly sins—and I'm already going to hell for mine.

I go to his room, knocking softly on the door. It's only a minute or so of me standing there when the door swings open and I'm face to face with an annoyed Reece.

He doesn't even say hello, instead, he snaps, "What are you doing here, Jasp?"

I don't give him a greeting in return. "I had to see you after last night," I admit, feeling my cheeks heat with the recall in my mind of what we did together.

"Yeah, well, I'm busy. About to head out on a job."

"Oh, well I'll go then. I'm sorry I barged in."

I turn to leave but Reece grabs my arm and pulls me back for an intense kiss.

Breaking the kiss, Reece asks, "How'd you find my room?"

"Asked a few people," I admit, blushing.

"You dickhead, Capullo," Reece berates, infuriated. "You think people don't know who you are."

I look down at my feet, not able to meet his annoyed glare when I confess, "I didn't think. I just wanted to see you."

"Well, that was stupid," he taunts. He shakes his head, scoffing. "Now I gotta sneak you out."

"I'm sorry," I stammer, giving him a death glare. "You left without a word during the night after you violated me."

He scoffs again. "You fucking loved it."

"Fine, I did, but I hated that it was you who gave me that pleasure."

"The greatest pleasure comes from hate, Jasper," Reece rasps, picking up his gun, and tucking it into the side of his jeans.

"Is that the same gun?"

"Only one I have."

"Was it um?" I question, not sure of the words that are stuck on the tip of my tongue.

"Um what, Jasper? Use your words," Reece taunts.

I seethe, annoyed that he's taunting me when he knows exactly what I'm asking him.

"Was it loaded last night when you used it in me?"

Reece shakes his head, a smirk upturning the corner of his mouth.

"I may be a monster, but I didn't fuck you with a loaded gun, Capullo. I put the safety on anyway out of habit."

"Oh ok good," I mumble, feeling like an idiot for asking.

Reece's smirk becomes wider, and he quirks his eyebrow. "Want me to?"

I gulp and Reece kisses me without warning. "Don't be scared, Jasp. You gotta trust me," Reece taunts, winking at me.

"I don't trust you. I hate you."

"I hate you too, and right now you're going to cause me to hate you more if I'm late for this job."

"Oh," I gasp, shifting aside, my eyes catching on something moving under the covers of the bed behind Reece.

"Reece, something is moving in your bed," I inform him pointing towards the small mound that's just covered.

Reece laughs as a black cat emerges, stretching its front paws out, and arching its back.

"Oh, it's just my boy, Raven."

Reece picks him up, petting it in long strokes from its head to the end of its tail. The cat likes the touch, leaning into Reece's hand.

He holds him out towards me, teasing, "Say hello to my pussy, Capullo."

I shrink back shrieking, "Get that thing away from me! Cats scare me."

Raven hisses, his black eyes staring me down as he stretches out his claws to lunge at me.

"Eeek, he's attacking me!" I shriek, stepping backwards to get away from the beast.

Reece laughs again, tipping his head down to kiss the cat's head. "He likes you," he says to me before asking the cat, "don't you Rave?"

The cat miaows, and licks Reece's fingers as he puts him back down on the bed.

He takes my hand then, yanking me out the door.

"We have to go, Jasp. And seeing as you're not leaving of your own accord you're coming with me."

I gasp in shock, barely able to stay upright as we're rushing through the hallway, me being dragged by Reece hastily until we're out in the car park and Reece shoves me into the passenger seat of his Bugatti.

CHAPTER TWENTY-ONE

REECE

*J*asper grips the door handle in a death hold, not saying a word as we drive across town. You'd think I was driving him off a cliff with his reaction.

Quickly arriving at the pub, I drag Jasper inside, hoping no one saw us. He's already put his foot in it by asking about me at uni, so word is probably going to get around that a guy from the rich side of town was asking about me and was seen with me. Thankfully, Malyk is at the pub. I shove Jasper towards the bar and he sits on a stool whilst I pull Malyk aside. He laughs and taunts me, "Ooo, dropping off your boy toy for me to play with, Ree."

Watching Jasper out of the corner of my eye I respond with malice, "Touch him, and I'll slice you open to bleed out without a care, Malyk."

Malyk laughs again, elbowing me in the side so I focus my attention on him and not Jasper.

"You've got it bad for thy enemy, my sweet," Malyk teases.

I grip Malyk's neck, shoving him against the wall, seething into his face, "I hate Jasper Capullo."

Malyk chuckles like a hyena again. I swear he laughs that way to piss me off, knowing it grates on my nerves. "Keep telling yourself that, my sweet. You're walking the line."

"Shut ya trap Malyk or I'll shut it for you."

I let go, and Malyk nods over to Jasper sitting at the bar sipping on a glass of clear liquid.

"Your boy looks so pretty wrapping his lips around that glass," Malyk comments, licking his lips.

"What're you implying Mal?" I question him, balling my fists so I don't hit him.

Malyk smirks, laughing loudly. "I bet those lips look pretty as fuck wrapped around your thick cock," he taunts with a moan. I see red. But also I see images of that very thing in my mind—knowing exactly what that feels like—and my dick twitches in my jeans.

"Don't Mal," I warn. "Don't even think those thoughts about him, nor my cock.

Malyk's eyes light up. "So has he sucked you off?"

I scoff, flipping Malyk off. "I gotta go," I tell him, heading out the door when I tell him, "Look after him but don't touch what's mine."

Malyk laughs and then scoffs, teasing me, "I'm kinky my sweet but I don't have a death wish."

He flips me off too, sauntering over to Jasper and standing behind him, leaning in. My stomach twists, and for a moment I consider going over to Jasper and kissing him, to send the message home to my best friend that Jasper is really mine. But I'm already late for this job and despite his teasing, I trust Malyk to keep his hands to himself. If he doesn't I won't hesitate to follow through on my threat.

Jasper Capullo is mine.

Heading out to the back of the pub, I climb on the motorbike I'd stashed there for quick jobs when I didn't want someone recognising the Bugatti. I slide my helmet on and speed off to the docks, crossing into Capullo territory. Pressing down on the pedal I can feel my knife against my ankle where it's tucked into my boot.

I'm wondering if I'll get the chance to use it on this job.

Getting to the docks, I park the bike, just out of sight and leave my helmet on the seat. Sliding off, I grab my gun out and start stalking around with the gun cocked looking for the hit. It doesn't take more than a few minutes before I find 'him' unloading boxes from the back of a shipping container.

"Drop the boxes, Maxwell."

The idiot drops the box on his foot, cursing and clutching it as he turns around to face me, trepidation and anxiety painted on his ugly mug.

"I…I'm innocent," he stammers, warily taking a few steps back.

I chuckle, and it bounces off the walls. "More like guilty. Where are you planning on taking this coke? Back to Montserrat territory?"

He's been doing dodgy dealings for months, bringing cocaine and other illicit drugs back into Montserrat territory–mainly to my father's club– which is forbidden in my father's fucked up club rules.

"No…taking it for myself. I swear."

"So you're stealing?" I taunt him, holding my gun out so it's pointing at his chest.

Maxwell stutters, "No…no…I would never steal."

Again I laugh and taunt him more, "Seems you're a liar and a petty thief like those you work for."

He gulps, shuffling back even further into the shipping container.

"I'm not…please…just let me go."

I laugh maniacally. "You know what I do to liars and thieves, Maxwell?"

He shakes his head, and I step closer to him, pressing the gun to the side of his head. His whole body is shaking. I could pull the trigger, and end him right then and there, but there's no fun in that. A quick kill is no fun.

"No. Please," Maxwell begs, his tone pathetic.

"Are you begging me to blow your brains out the side of your head, all over this shipping container?"

"Please…don't. I'll do anything."

I press the gun against his skull harder leaning in to taunt him, "Anything huh?"

"Yeah anything, just don't kill me."

"On your knees then. Suck my dick whilst I hold this loaded gun to your head."

He scoffs, shaking his head violently and causing the gun to move. "No. I'm not sucking a guy's dick. Anything but that."

I laugh again. "You said anything, Maxwell. Did you lie again? Did you not mean your words?"

"I didn't lie. But…"

I cut him off, "But you did."

I push him down onto his knees, taunting with malice in my tone, "Your choice, Maxwell. Suck or die?"

I shove my pelvis against Maxwell's face. I'm barely hard. And don't want Maxwell to actually suck me. He spits on my jeans.

"Fuck you!" he hisses at me.

"You'd love that, wouldn't you? But that wasn't an option."

I grip Maxwell's hair and tilt his head up, drawing the trigger back.

"Seems you've made your choice."

I fire the gun and the blood spatters, the bullet flying through his head and hitting the side of the shipping container with a loud clink. Shoving Maxwell to the floor, I kick him down and spit on him.

"Capullo scum."

Leaning down I wipe the blood off my gun on Maxwell's t-shirt, kicking him one last time before I leave and get on my bike again to go back to the pub. That was an easy kill, but it messed with my head. He was the enemy, just like Jasper is and that is causing my head to spin.

CHAPTER TWENTY-TWO

Jasper

'm playing pool with Malyk when Reece comes stalking back into the pub. He looks wound up, as though the weight of the world is on his shoulders. He steps up behind me whilst I'm taking a shot. I stand stock still, my cue resting on the edge of the table as I line it up.

Reece leans in to whisper in my ear, "Did he touch you?"

I shake my head, turning slightly so we're nearly kissing. "No," I respond.

Reece pushes his pelvis against my butt, taunting me, "You better not be lying to me, Capullo." My breath hitches. There's malice in Reece's tone, and it's causing my pulse to race.

Malyk laughs from across the pool table, turning our attention.

"Go fuck each other," he jeers.

Stifling a laugh, I stab my cue back, taking my turn. I've barely hit the ball with the cue tip when

Reece grabs my hand to drag me away, taking me outside. He shoves me against the wall, kissing me hard and unforgiving. It's a bruising kiss, demanding as he forces his tongue into my mouth to deepen the kiss causing me to groan into his mouth.

With a desperate panting gasp Reece pulls back.

"Did Malyk touch you?" He questions touching my lips with his thumb, and I lick it. "Kiss you? Flirt with you?"

I shake my head. "He might be my best friend but I won't hesitate to hurt anyone that touches what's mine," I growl.

"No," I reply, exhaling and admitting, "I don't want him."

"Who do you want, Capullo?"

"No one," I blurt out, focusing on the ground instead of meeting Reece's intense gaze. He's going to know I'm lying if he sees the blush on my cheeks.

"Liar," Reece murmurs.

"Arsehole," I snap back, snidely.

"You know what I do to liars, Jasper?" Reece rasps.

I shake my head. "No," I admit, reaching out and touching his side where his gun is stashed. "But it probably has something to do with your gun."

Reece smirks. "Smart boy," he jeers. "But it's not always a gun I kill with."

I gasp, questioning him, "No?" I don't know if I want him to answer me. I do have an idea but I want to hear Reece say it.

"No, sometimes I like to draw blood with a flick of my knife across skin."

"Knife? Like you slapped my butt with?" I question.

Reece steps back bending down and withdrawing his knife from his boot. He runs it over his finger, the tip biting his finger for a droplet of blood. He puts the finger to my lip.

"Lick it, Capullo."

"No, I'm not sucking your blood off your finger," I tell him, pouting and shaking my head.

"So defiant," Reece taunts, pushing his finger into my mouth. I can't help but lick it, and it causes me to moan.

Reece pulls his finger out, smirking at me, and praising, "Good boy."

"Stop calling me that. It's patronising."

Reece scoffs, then taunts, "You demand that like I care."

He holds up the knife against my neck and tilts my head back.

"Reece..." I drawl out his name, gasping for breath. "Don't. Hurt. Me."

He presses the knife against my neck a little harder, drawing the blade across so it slices a thin cut that starts to bleed. I know it's not deep, not life threatening but still I let out a raspy breath, panting, "Reece."

"Fuck, you look so pretty bleeding for me, Capullo."

Reece drops the knife, and tips my neck back more, licking from my collarbone up my neck and chin to then kiss me. I moan against his lips, tasting the blood on his tongue and lips. "Reece, fuck. More," I moan against his lips, only just breaking the kiss.

"More? You want more, Capullo?"

"Yes. Yes," I pant, and Reece licks up my neck again kissing me harder than before. He shoves his hand into the front of my sweats, breaking the kiss, and staring at me when he grips my neck in his palm.

"You wearing lacy underwear, Capullo?" He asks, his eyes lighting up.

"Yes," I admit, feeling myself blush as I add, "I… like how it feels."

"Fuck, Jasper that's hot," Reece rasps, staring at me as he shoves his hand back into my sweats and starts palming my dick over my undies.

"Reece…" I groan.

"Yeah, Jasper. You're going to come for me. Dirty up your sexy lacy underwear."

He kisses me again, sliding his hand into my underwear, stroking my dick and teasing the tip with his finger.

"Reece, stop, stop," I moan, bucking my hips forward for more friction. It feels so good. I don't really want him to stop, but the words fell from my lips anyway.

Reece squeezes my balls, asking, "You want me to stop?"

"Yes. No. It feels too good."

Reece laughs, stroking down towards my taint.

"Oh fuck!" I bellow, my orgasm hitting out of nowhere, causing me to moan as my come soaks my sweats and undies.

Reece yanks out his hand, and it's practically clean. "You dick, leaving me no cream on my hand to taste."

I look down at my crotch, biting back, "You arse! You made me come all over myself."

Reece smirks. "You look sexy covered in come, Capullo."

"I hate you, Montserrat," I spit at him.

Reece sniggers. "You didn't hate me touching you though." He's right but I don't admit that to him.

"Fuc…" I stammer, not able to complete my train of thought as Reece cuts me off with a kiss, yanking my sweats down at the same time causing me to break the kiss with a shocked, annoyed gasp.

"So damn pretty," Reece taunts crouching down and licking my dick through the lace, and moaning with each swipe of his tongue. I grip his hair, fisting it tightly as I request, "Suck me please, Reece."

Reece stands, scoffing. "You don't get to ask that of me, Capullo."

"I hate you," I rage at him. "I hate that you take and demand, and cause me to sin over and over."

Reece laughs. "Sinning feels so good, Jasper. And if what we do together is sinning then send me to hell."

I let out an exasperated sigh. "You're from hell, Montserrat. The devil in the flesh."

Reece steps away with a smirk on his face.

"Come back to the dorm with me, Jasper and I'll take you to heaven," he hums, his Adam's Apple vibrating. It's kinda sexy.

He doesn't wait for my response, instead he goes inside, and I huff as I yank up my now soaked sweats annoyed at myself for again giving into Reece and for loving his depravity.

CHAPTER TWENTY-THREE

REECE

*J*asper had quickly followed me back inside the pub. I'd stared him down, whilst finishing the game of pool we'd abandoned with Malyk and now we're back in my dorm room lying on my bed.

Jasper's sweats have a huge come stain on the front, and I smirk at him, teasing him, "You're such a dirty boy, coming all over yourself."

He glares up at me, as I yank them down. "It's your fault. You're always touching me."

"You love it, Capullo."

"I don't. I hate it. Hate you," he snarls at me and fuck it's sexy.

"That's it. Bare those teeth and snarl for me, pretty boy." He grits his teeth, obeying me and letting out a dirty snarl that resembles a moan.

CAZ MAY

"Such a good boy, Capullo," I taunt, gripping his lacy dry come crusted underwear and ripping them.

"Hey!" he screams at me, annoyed.

"They were crusty, Jasp. Just doing you a favour."

He's giving me the most annoyed glare. Angry Jasper is sexy as hell. And honestly I never–well barely ever–give rather than receive oral, but seeing Jasper's hardening cock between the lace is a glorious sight. And that's not even mentioning the way he's looking at me like he's begging for it.

Leaning over him I kiss him, and he moans into my mouth, his dick hardening between us and brushing against my thigh. It excites me that I can get him this hard with just kisses, and can make him come without a touch.

Without giving him any indication of my plans I slide down the bed and pry his thighs open so I can kneel in between them. Leaning down I slowly take his cock into my mouth, laving my tongue over his length.

"Fuck, Reece," he moans bucking his hips up, causing his dick to push further down my throat. The tip hits the roof of my mouth causing me to gag and pulling out I murmur, "damn you've got a nice cock, Capullo."

I continue to suck him off until he spills down my throat in a hot spurt. I swallow his load down and rest my head on his stomach for a moment, glancing up at him as he pants for breath.

"Thank you for that," Jasper pants, inhaling a deep breath.

I sit up, crossing my legs and laughing. "You don't have to thank me for sex, weirdo."

Jasper sneers. "You're just always taking from me, Reece."

"I'm sorry," I murmur, not able to meet his gaze as he sits up against the headboard and stares at me with a frown. "I don't mean to be that way. It's just always been that way with the guys I've been with." I'm putting myself out there with that statement. Admitting to him that I know I'm a selfish arsehole. It's fucking ridiculous but it hurts like I'm stabbing myself in the heart with my knife, knowing I'm hurting Jasper with my actions. I shouldn't care less, but for some fucked up reason I do.

He bites down on his lip, mumbling something incoherent before he sighs.

"Well, I haven't been with another guy," he admits, dropping his gaze so he's not looking at me when he adds, "Just you."

"So you've never dated anyone?" I ask, causing him to glance up at me, his eyes covered by his hair flopping in his face.

"No," he admits. "And we're not dating Reece."

"True," I respond, still just staring at him.

He gives me an incredulous look before I lean forward, covering his body with mine and kissing him. He surrenders to the kiss, licking my lips and biting my upper lip as he moans into my mouth. After kissing for a few minutes, he gasps for air and murmurs softly when I pull back. "Kissing you feels amazing Reece," he confesses, his cheeks colouring.

"Am I the only person you've kissed?" I ask him with a smirk.

I'm guessing his answer will be yes, but Jasper shakes his head. "No, I've kissed a few people," he admits, his cheeks darkening. His shyness is coming out, and fuck it's sexy.

I scoot across the bed, so I'm sitting at his side, and I grip his cut jaw to bring his lips back to mine for another kiss. He again gives in, not able to get enough as he moans so loudly I'm sure everyone in the dorms can hear.

"Am I the only guy you've kissed?" I question after breaking the kiss. This time I'm unsure of what his answer will be.

Jasper kisses me, stealing my breath and murmuring against my lips, "Yes."

I fully break the kiss, my forehead against his. I'm about to respond when he interjects shyly, "And you're the best kisser ever.

I groan at his admission, closing the space between us by kissing Jasper harder and deeper. "Mmm, Jasp," I moan against his lips. "I guess I'll need to kiss you more then."

The corner of his mouth quirks up, and he replies, "I wouldn't be opposed to that."

He shifts to move away from me, off the bed, his demeanour taking a complete one-eighty and the opposite of his words. "But I have to go now," he stammers, his legs over the edge of my bed.

"You could stay," I say more as a statement than a question, shocking myself.

"I don't think we're at that point, Reece. I barely know you."

"We don't need to know each other's whole lives to kiss and make each other come."

Jasper blushes, his gaze only just on me when he admits softly, "You're the only person who's made me come."

"Fuck Jasp," I curse loudly, grabbing his hands and pulling him back onto the bed. "That's hot."

I kiss him again, rolling over so I'm straddling him again. Staring straight into his eyes–taking in his stunned expression–I grip his dick and start slowly stroking it.

A drop of precum pearls in his slit, and he moans, "Reece...feels...good."

I don't say anything, instead, I thrust forward so my dick slides up his, my precum coating his velvety skin. Letting go of his dick a moment, I wrap my hand around both of our cocks, once more stroking his length. And this time I'm fucking my hand, my cock slipping along his, our precum covering us both as lube.

"Reece!" he calls out as he comes hard with his whole body shaking. He's covered my hand and his stomach, and looks up at me as though he's drunk, mumbling, "I...I love it when you make me come, Reece."

His words spur me on, and I come then, spurting out ropes of come across his stomach. I swipe my hand through the come on Jasper's stomach and put my fingers into his mouth to feed it to him.

"Mmm," Jasper moans, causing me to groan.

"You're so fucking sexy, pretty boy," I tell him before leaning down and licking the rest of the come off his stomach. Once I'm satisfied I've cleaned every last drop off his abs I give Jasper another kiss. I could kiss him night and day, until the end of damn time and that would never be enough. He's insatiable.

"I really should go now. I've got heaps of homework."

I want to tell him to stay, to sleep in my bed with me, but this time he's standing from the bed at lightning speed. He's pulling away, and I feel as though he's using me to explore his sexuality, to get off and nothing else. That shouldn't hurt. I've done the very thing to other guys, but it does hurt.

"Sneak out then," I tell him, laying down on my back and watching Jasper—and his gorgeous toned arse—as he dresses before he leaves without a word.

My mind wanders to him saying that we don't know each other. I want to get to know him, but it feels like Jasper isn't going to let me in to truly get to know him. The used feeling is sending my thoughts spiralling. Jasper Capullo has fucked me up. And it seems as though I might be falling for my enemy.

CHAPTER TWENTY-FOUR

Jasper

I have textbooks, notebooks and the entire contents of my pencil case sprawled out on my bed, in the thick of studying the Renaissance. The stupid essay I have to do analysing and comparing two artists' work from that period is doing my head in. I love art history, exploring different artwork from history and putting my spin on it, but I'm more practical–hands on–and I hate theory. Words on a page aren't my strong suit by any means. Give me a paintbrush and a blank canvas any day.

Hearing a knock on my door is a welcome distraction. Jumping up from the bed I leap across the floor–nearly falling flat on my face–as I rush to open it. My heart is pounding, hoping it's Reece. I shouldn't want to see him, but I do.

Opening the door, it's not Reece however, it's Nancy.

She glares at me, with a cheeky smirk as she barges into my room and I shut the door behind her. Rushing back over to my bed, I gather up my books and shove them aside.

Nancy sits on the edge of the bed, crossing her legs.

"What's with the late night visit, Nanc?" I question her, raising my eyebrow.

"I got us something, Jasp," she squeaks excitedly, still with the cheeky smirk.

"What Nanc?" I ask eagerly, due to her excited demeanour.

Reaching into her pocket she pulls out a tiny ziplock bag, with a couple of joints in it. She waves it in my face, and I shake my head. "Nanc, no, we haven't smoked in forever."

She chuckles and then opens the ziplock bag. "Then all the more reason to enjoy a hit."

Once more I shake my head at my best friend. "I shouldn't, Nancy. You know what weed does to me."

Nancy laughs. "Yes, my darling. It causes you to lose all inhibition and speak your truth."

"Exactly. And I don't want to face the truth right now." I sigh deeply.

"Don't be a sad sack," Nancy teases, pulling a lighter out of her pocket and lighting up one of the joints. She takes a drag of it and exhales, before holding it out to me. I'm pacing the room, feeling on edge at the thought of taking a drag.

Again I shake my head. "I can't, Nanc."

"Yes, you can Jasper," she encourages. "Stop pacing and sit your arse down, and take a damn drag."

I sigh, and sit cross legged in front of my best friend on the bed. Grabbing the joint from her fingers I take a long drag.

"Good boy, Jasp," Nancy teases.

I seethe at her, waving the lit joint in the air. "Don't fucking say that, Nanc. Fuck."

"Why?" She questions, glaring at me oddly, and sniggering.

"He...he says that to me."

"Who? Reece?"

I nod. "Yeah, and it's so fucking patronising. I fucking hate it."

Nancy's eyes light up and she giggles, asking, "Does he say it when you're fucking?"

"We haven't fucked, Nancy."

"You want to fuck him though?"

"Um...no," I murmur, taking another drag. Nancy is still giggling, so I admit, "I want him to fuck me."

Nancy laughs harder, teasing, "Whilst he tells you you're a good boy, huh?"

I blush. "It does sound different when he says it, and when he calls me pretty boy, it turns me on," I admit, feeling my cheeks darkening.

"Are you in love with him?" Nancy asks, taking another drag when I hand it back to her. Once more I shake my head.

"No, no, way, but his kisses, and his touch are like a drug to me. He's as addictive as this weed."

Nancy seems to have calmed. "I think you're in love with him, Jasp."

"No, I'm so not, he's bad for me, Nanc. He does being bad so well, but he's not the guy for me."

"Don't discount your feelings for him because he's the enemy, Jasp."

"I'm not," I scoff. "I don't have feelings for him," I chuckle, and then add as I'm taking another drag. "This is good shit."

"I know right," Nancy responds with a laugh and we fall back on the bed laughing like crazy.

"I'm such a bad boy." I chuckle. "If Dad could see me now, he'd kill me."

"Your dad is blind, Jasp. He has no idea you're not his good boy."

"Nope," I reply, laughing madly and sitting up. "I wanna go for a swim," I announce.

"Now? It's dark, Jasp."

"Don't care. I'm doing it."

I stand, stripping down to my boxers, and grabbing a towel. I'm out the door in barely a minute. Nancy runs after me, calling out, "Jasp! You're crazy!"

"Yep!" I yell. "You coming?"

"You're on your own, bestie," Nancy says calmly as she heads to her car.

Getting in her car she drives off as I run across the road.

"Be careful!" She calls out her window, driving past me. I give her a thumbs up and run onto the sand of Vemore Bay beach.

Throwing my towel on the sand, I run into the waves and dive beneath them. Coming up, I inhale a gulp of air and push up from the sand beneath my feet so I'm floating on my back looking up at the night sky.

My mind wanders to Reece, the way he last made me feel. There's something about Reece Montserrat that causes me to give in to temptation every damn time. I can't help myself. I crave the sin.

Closing my eyes, I let my mind drift to thoughts of Reece's kiss on my lips, his tongue teasing the forbidden places that only he's seen. I can't believe I've let him get me naked so many times now, and that it hasn't bothered me. I haven't felt the need to hide my body from him. I'm also surprised at myself for loving his naked body, and how his skin is covered in tattoos, even up to his neck. I think about the rose and spiderwebs on his neck, and the intricacy of them and his other tattoos. They're art on his skin that shows outwardly the torment of his mind.

It's blissful being out in the ocean, my high from the weed slowly wearing off as I float towards the rocks. A sudden current pushes me closer to them and bumping into them I screech in pain, my side hitting some jagged rocks. It slices my side—just above my hip—and it's quite deep.

Wincing I push myself out of the water, up onto the rocks to inspect the damage. It's bleeding—and because my high is wearing off—it hurts, badly. The saltwater is causing it to sting.

Stumbling over the rocks I grab my towel from the sand, pressing it against the cut to curb the blood.

"Fuck," I hiss, rushing back to the dorms, cursing the entire time from the pain.

The moment I'm back in my dorm room I send a pic in just my boxers to Nancy,

You let me go swimming whilst high

You say that like I could have stopped you, you arse! Does it hurt?

Like a bitch.

Go find Reece...he'll kiss you better

Groaning, I put my phone down, pulling the covers back from my bed and sliding under the sheets.

Reece wouldn't kiss me better, he'd kiss the cut, tongue it—savouring the taste of my blood— as he licks the blood and wound clean. I hate that the thought of Reece doing that is turning me on. That I want that very thing to happen. My head is filled with those thoughts as I close my eyes drifting to sleep.

I slide my hand into my boxers and start palming my dick. I'm hard, and moaning in mere seconds, slipping my hand up and down my dick. I've never touched myself before and I'm taken aback by how good it feels—with thoughts of Reece in my head— as I tease the tip of my dick with my finger. I'm toying with the edge of sleep when my hips shake and I come in my boxers before I sigh and succumb to the sleep that's pulling me under. I have no idea if I'll wake up tomorrow, or if I'll bleed out from the cut. It would be my payment for my depraved sins and thoughts.

CHAPTER TWENTY-FIVE

Jasper

I wake up with a start the next morning, expecting Reece to be in my bed as my thoughts were filled with him last night to the point I could've sworn he was right next to me, sucking my dick. My boxers are dry but crusty from coming in them, and I've yanked them down at some point during the night as my sheets are also covered in come. I know what that means and it worries me that behaviour—my condition—has caused a night of of restlessness that ends in a dirty bed.

Getting up, I kick the crusty boxers aside and grab a clean pair out of my drawers as well as some denim shorts and a black t-shirt. Tugging them on I wince from the pain in my side. It's still smarting from the cut. Thankfully it's not bleeding anymore.

Before heading out the door, I pull on my sneakers and grab my car keys. I need to see Reece—to tell him about my depraved dreams of him—and how the very thought of him gets me hard.

There's only one place I can think he'd be. The pub in Montserrat territory that he took me to. I'm petrified—driving there—as I hear gunshots in the street, and see people behaving indecently in the street in broad daylight as though that's not illegal. This side of Vemore is a world away.

I slide my Aston Martin into a car park right outside the pub, and getting out I press the lock button repeatedly to ensure it's locked before I pocket my keys and head inside.

Glancing around the pub, it doesn't take long to know that Reece is not at the pub. I feel deflated, and upset. I'm about to turn on my heels and leave when I hear my name being called out from across the room, "Jasper!"

It's Malyk, and he sidles up next to me, hip bumping me.

"Oh...ah, hi Malyk," I stammer.

"Hello to you, Jasper. You here for Reece?"

"Ah yeah...is he here?"

"Nah, he's gone out on a job," Malyk informs me and again I turn away towards the door to leave.

Malyk stops me, gripping my arm and yanking me back towards him so our bodies collide.

"You don't have to leave, sexy."

"I...um...I...Reece," I stammer, completely lost for words. I don't like this. Don't like the feeling of Malyk's hand on my bare arm, his body against mine. My body doesn't react to him, at all.

I wrench myself from the grip he has on my arm, taking a step back as I request, "Please leave me be, Malyk. I'm not attracted to you. You know what Reece will do if he sees us this close"

Malyk chuckles, annoyingly. "But you're attracted to Ree?"

My cheeks heat. "Well, yeah," I admit, turning my gaze away from Malyk's. Again he laughs, his tone odd, protective when he asks, "Do you love him?"

"No, I don't know. I know I feel something for him, yes, but it's not love?" I say more like a question.

Malyk nods. "It may be so," he says with a knowing smile. "He looks at you every time you look away."

I shake my head, not wanting to believe that Malyk's words are truthful. Reece has given me the impression that his best friend harbours feelings for him, so it's odd that he'd be pushing me towards Reece if that were so.

"There is no way Reece loves me," I respond.

Malyk chuckles, his tone teasing when he says, "Don't be sure about that, lovely."

I push for more, needing to hear him affirm his words in another way with different words. "You think he loves me?"

Malyk nods, winking at me. "I'd almost count on it, Jasper. Reece is different around you," he tells me.

"Different? How so?"

"You've fucked him up. In a good way."

I gasp, not sure what to make of that bold statement. "Oh, well despite the sin we've committed together, being around him makes me happy," I admit, my cheeks heating again with the confession and acknowledgement of my sins out loud.

"And I'm sure my best friend feels the same about you. The fact you're enemies be damned."

"Yeah," I agree. "I should go. Please tell him I dropped by when you see him."

Malyk nods affirming he'll follow through with my request. "Does he have your phone number?" he asks.

I shake my head, taking my phone out of my pocket. "No, we haven't exchanged numbers."

"Let me put his number in your phone," Malyk suggests.

Hesitantly I hand my phone over and Malyk adds in Reece's number. "I put it under Lover boy, and shot off a text of an eggplant and a kiss emoji."

Taking my phone back I laugh to hide the nervousness of Reece seeing that message. "Thanks, Malyk."

"No worries, catch ya later, gorgeous." I don't respond to that. It's clear that Malyk calls everyone endearing pet names. I leave, staring at the open message on my phone—as I head out the door—to see Reece has read the text but hasn't replied. His lack of response hurts. It shows me Malyk is full of shit in regards to Reece's feelings for me. I should just forget about Reece Montserrat, but that is easier said than done. He's under my skin, in my head and I wish he'd leave me be.

CHAPTER TWENTY-SIX

REECE

After another job–I'd rather forget–I get back to the pub.

I'm vexed with Malyk. The guy is always overstepping boundaries.

I wave my phone in his face as I step up to the bar where he's sitting, sipping on a bourbon.

"Who are you sending my number to again, fucker?" I ask, more as a demand.

"Just your lover boy," he responds with his signature smirk.

"Huh?" I respond because surely he's not referring to the enemy.

"Don't be so daft, my sweet," he taunts, taking a sip of his bourbon and sniggering under his breath.

"You sent my number to Capullo?"

"Yeah, your boy came here to see you. He was frothing at the mouth."

"What the fuck Mal?" I snap, disgruntled that he'd do that behind my back.

Malyk laughs. "He wants you, Ree. The boy is pining for you big time."

"So, what are you saying?"

"That you both need to get off your high horses and admit your feelings to each other."

I scoff, signalling the bartender for a drink. "You know that's not possible Mal. Our families will disown us, plus did you forget I hate Jasper."

"Do you?" he taunts, sniggering again. "Do you really hate him? Or do you hate that he makes you feel?"

"I hate him, but that's not all I feel for him," I admit, sighing and taking a sip of the whiskey the bartender slides down the bar towards me. That's a perk about coming to this pub regularly, the bar staff know our poison without asking.

Gulping the bitter liquid down, I sigh again, admitting, "He makes me feel alive in a whole new way."

Malyk chuckles, eyeing me over the rim of his glass. "My sweet, you don't hate him. You love him."

"The fuck I do," I snap, spitting some of my whiskey towards my best friend in my huff.

"Just be with him. Let your guard down," Malyk tells me with a condescending tone.

"I've done that, but I get the feeling he's not completely letting me in."

"Then get him to. Fuck it out of him."

For some fucked up reason I blush at that suggestion and look away.

"Have you not fucked him?" Malyk asks, quirking his eyebrow at me.

"No," I admit, feeling my cheeks heating more. My feeling this way about sex is weird. "We've done everything except fuck. I think he's pure."

"Seriously? You think he's a virgin?"

"He's practically said so," I tell my best friend with a nod. "But I don't know whether to believe him."

"Yeah, damn."

"Right," I acknowledge. "There's no way a guy as gorgeous as Jasper is still a virgin."

"Yep, but if so, you need to take his cherry, Ree. Make his gorgeous arse yours alone."

I nod, sniggering. "I'm going to ruin the sweet Jasper Capullo."

Malyk laughs and mumbles something that I can't hear, but I think it's, 'and you'll fall for him, completely.'

I down the rest of my whiskey, slamming the glass down on the bar top before I leave the pub. I text Jasper on the way out.

Capullo, my pretty boy

Are you mad?

Not at you. But Malyk is a dead man walking.

Don't hurt your best friend.

You want me to hurt you instead?

No 😊

You at the dorms?

Yeah, why?

I'm coming over.

😬

I just wanna hear about your day and make you cum, pretty boy

Um ok...are you horny?

No, you're just so damn sexy all the time, Jasp

Oh ok...

I wanna make you moan.

I want you in my mouth

Fuck Capullo, I type, hastily getting in my car and speeding off, desperate to get to the dorms.

CHAPTER TWENTY-SEVEN

Jasper

I t's barely been fifteen minutes since I messaged Reece, and he's knocking–rather loudly–on my dorm room door.

Opening it to him, he barges in and I glance down the hallway to see if anyone is around. The coast appears clear, but I can't shake the on edge feeling and Reece senses it, asking with a teasing lilt, "Why are you so worried, Jasp?"

"Did anyone see you?" I ask, closing the door behind me.

"No, seriously relax," Reece responds, reaching out to touch my abs through my t-shirt causing me to wince as his fingers graze my cut.

"You ok? Is that blood on your t-shirt?" Reece questions, his eyes caught on the streak of red I've only just noticed on my white t-shirt.

"Yes, no," I reply, shrinking back from him.

He glares at me, his eyes darkening with rage. "What happened Jasper? Did someone hurt you?" His tone softens with the second question, a protectiveness in his tone that causes my heart to race as I sit on the edge of my bed. Reece follows, sitting on the edge and glaring at me, awaiting my response.

I feel like an idiot, admitting, "I went swimming last night, whilst I was high and cut my side on some jagged rocks."

Reece gasps. "Shit, sounds like that would've hurt."

I bite down on his lip. "Ah, yeah. It did."

"Show me," Reece requests suddenly, gripping the hem of my t-shirt and yanking it up. His eyes take in the cut, studying every tear in my lightly tanned skin. It's still throbbing a little, but I'm trying not to think of that, and the sting of pain.

"Damn, Capullo you certainly did a number on yourself."

"Yeah, I um…I…"

"What?"

"I nearly messaged you to come over and kiss me better, but I was still coming down from my high and I fell asleep," I tell him, feeling my cheeks heating more and more with each word.

Reece chuckles. "You should of," he says, adding with a snigger, "And I can't imagine you high."

"It was only weed. Nancy bought it over for a bit of fun because I've been so uptight lately."

"Well, that's not something I expected from you, at all. Thought you were a proper good boy," Reece teases, smirking at me.

"I am," I counter. "But a good boy can have a bit of fun too."

"Yeah, dirty fun," Reece sniggers.

He leans forward and kisses me, edging my t-shirt up a little, and brushing his fingers over the bottom of the wound.

"Take it off, Jasp," he requests, nodding towards my t-shirt in his grip.

I pull my t-shirt off, throwing it on the floor. Reece kisses me hard, and fast before then trailing kisses down my abs.

"I fucking love your body, Jasper," he comments, licking each nipple, causing me to writhe and moan. "You're so fucking sexy."

He kisses each ridge of my abs, pinching my nipples at the same time.

"Fuck, Reece, stop," I groan, bucking my hips up. "God it feels so good."

"Mmm…you don't want me to stop?" Reece taunts, running his tongue along the wound.

"No. More, Reece. More," I beg.

Reece is still pinching my nipples and he runs his tongue along the wound more, licking the cut flesh whilst moaning. "Mmm, Capullo, your blood tastes so sweet."

"Reece, fuck. What are you doing to me?"

Reece laughs. "Edging you, pretty boy," he taunts.

"That's so cruel, Reece."

"It will be worth it, Jasper," he promises me as he starts licking down over my cut lines. I buck my hips up, to meet his lips, moaning, "Reeeece."

He yanks my boxers off, tugging them off at my ankles before he licks my inner thighs, spreading my legs wider. "Mmm...feels good. Please, Reece."

"Please what, pretty boy?"

"Suck me," I request, my voice a muted rasp.

"You demanding something of me, Capullo?"

Reece looks up, his glare angry. I shake my head. "No. I would never. I just want to come."

"And you will, but only if you're a good boy."

He licks my pucker then, just one wave of his tongue before he pulls back.

"Reece, please, I need to come."

He stretches up to kiss my lips, reaching down and teasing my hole with his fingers whilst kissing me.

The pleasure is coursing through my whole body, causing my hips to buck up. Reece slides another finger in, and I let out a squeal.

"Fuck. Reece. Please make me come."

He keeps fingering me and kissing me. My release hits, covering Reece's clothes in my come.

"You came all over me, dirty fucker."

"I hate you," I respond laughing.

"I hate you too," Reece reciprocates, standing and yanking off his clothes before he climbs into bed with me. He kisses me again before we lie back and I sigh.

"What's that sigh for?"

"I hate having to sneak around with you. Only able to be with you behind closed doors," I admit, huffing loudly.

"You know we can't be out, Jasp. The feud with our families makes us enemies."

"I know, but our parents' feud is not ours. I don't even know what they're fighting for." I don't say anything about his comment about us being enemies. He doesn't feel like my enemy anymore. He never did.

"Me either," Reece replies.

I yawn then, tiredness hitting me hard.

"Go to sleep, pretty boy," Reece coaxes as I roll over and Reece pulls me close, kissing the side of my head. It's a comforting gesture—not at all like his usual manner—and I murmur, loving the feeling of being cradled in Reece's embrace.

He's an enigma, hard and rough when it comes to sex—even with his words—but there's a sweetness underneath the outward persona. A sweetness that I'm wondering if he only shows me.

As I drift to sleep I contemplate my feelings for Reece. And I'm pretty damn sure I'm falling for him. Frankly, I'm probably in love with him, but I'm scared to admit that to myself, let alone voice it to him.

CAZ MAY

CHAPTER TWENTY-EIGHT

REECE

olting awake I roll over a little, shifting away from the still sleeping Jasper. He murmurs softly, and it sends a shiver down my spine.

I watch him—stare at him—my mind wandering to the night before and Jasper submitting to me without a protest. That turns me on, but now my dick is hardening from just watching him sleep. It's been a while since that's happened and I know I shouldn't but I flip back the covers to grip my hard dick, still staring at the sleeping Jasper. He's snoring softly, and his dick is twitching as he moves a little in his sleep.

I move so I'm kneeling in between Jasper's spread legs. It's as though he's letting me in without even knowing. I fist my dick, slowly starting to stroke my length. Precum is pearling on the tip and running my finger through it I coat my dick with it to jerk off harder and faster. Jasper is sighing in his sleep and it's causing my dick to harden even more. Watching him is turning me on so much my dick hurts in the best way. Still jerking my dick, I watch Jasper until I'm moaning and coming all over his naked sleeping body.

I'm loud, my moans reverberating around the dorm room and waking Jasper up, just as I'm squeezing the tip of my dick for the final drops of come to cover his skin.

He gasps. "Are you hard?" He questions, glancing down at his abs and stomach covered in come. "Did you just come on me whilst I was asleep?"

He looks horrified. I chuckle. "Yeah, I was jerking off and didn't want to wake you."

Jasper scoffs in disgust. "Eww, Reece. That's creepy as hell."

"You looked so peaceful and so damn sexy, it turned me on so much," I admit, shifting so I'm sitting next to his feet.

"I was asleep, Reece," Jasper comments, his voice laced with disgust.

"I know. I didn't want to wake you, but I needed to come," I confess, my hand gripping his calf. I don't know why I need to touch him. Maybe for some reassurance that I haven't overstepped an invisible line.

"I wouldn't have minded if you woke me," Jasper comments, his voice hesitant and nervous.

"I know that now," I respond laughing, adding with hesitation, unable to look at him, "But also I…"

"You what?" Jasper interrupts.

I sigh, and then admit, "I get off on watching people sleep. It turns me on."

"Um ok…that's weird," Jasper comments, his tone snide and mocking. I don't like his tone, but I swallow down my annoyance with a gulp and tell him, "It's called somnophilia."

Jasper eyes me, as though he's thinking hard. I can practically hear the cogs turning in his head. "Have you done this before with someone else?"

I blush a little, hating that I'm about to admit a secret to Jasper. "Yeah with Malyk."

"But he's your best friend?" Jasper comments, his voice raspy with shock.

"Yeah, but we'd often sleep in the same bed and I'd watch him sleep when I was up with the thoughts in my head," I tell him, adding with a slight chuckle, "He honestly sleeps like the dead."

Jasper doesn't say anything. He's just staring at me. I continue my confession, "I'd pull his pants down and touch him without him waking. And I'd come all over him and when he did wake up he'd always think he'd come himself."

"Oh, like a wet dream?" Jasper asks, his innocence showing.

"Yeah. I've never told him the truth. And you're not going to breathe a word of it either. The fucker would take it the wrong way."

"I won't. Not for me to tell," Jasper points out, reaching up to run a finger over his lips as though he's zipping them closed.

"Have you ever had a wet dream, Capullo?" I ask, smirking at him. I'm intrigued to hear his response.

Jasper blushes. "Uh…yeah. I've um…kinda… I…" he starts to admit but I stop him from saying more by climbing onto his lap. I start licking the come off his abs, running my tongue over every ridge, not leaving a drop of come on his skin.

Once he is free of come on his body, I lean over him and then kiss him, hard and zealously.

I murmur against his mouth, my voice raspy, "Tell me all your dirty confessions, Jasper."

"I…I can't. I haven't even told Nancy how depraved I am," he stammers, his cheeks turning crimson. He turns his gaze from mine, dipping his head to hide.

I tip his head back up with a finger under his chin.

"You can tell me all your secrets, Jasper."

"I doubt that, Reece," he mocks snidely.

I lean in to kiss him again and he accepts the kiss with a languid moan. I whisper against his lips, "I promise I won't tell a soul of your depravity."

Jasper exhales into my mouth which is odd, but I love sharing his breath. It's as though he's giving me his soul and that's weirdly satisfying.

"I just want you so fucking bad," I remark breaking the kiss with a raspy breath.

Jasper blushes and confesses, "I wanna do things with you that I haven't done with anyone before."

Oh, the possibilities.

"Mmm....Jasper," I moan. "Sounds like the best kind of sin."

Once more I kiss him, my body over his as we writhe together on the bed. Our dicks are sliding doors, and Jasper moans into my mouth, his tongue licking my lips, and dancing with mine. His hips buck up and he breaks the kiss with a gasp as he comes without my touching him.

"Fuck Capullo," I rasp, shifting back so I can see that he's covered us both in cum. "That is so damn sexy when you come all over yourself without a touch."

Jasper blushes, biting down on his lips before he admits softly, "Only you can cause that."

"It's hot, Jasp," I respond kissing him before I start kissing down his collarbone, leaving hickeys against his lightly tanned skin.

I stare at the marks on his body. My marks.

"I'm going to leave hickeys all over your body in only the places I can see," I rasp.

Jasper groans as I kiss all down his abs, leaving hickeys all over his body. When I reach his stomach I lick all the come off, moaning as I enjoy every last drop.

After I've cleaned his skin of come, Jasper murmurs, "You're hard, baby."

I eye him, my heart tripping from the nickname. "Baby huh?" I taunt, smirking.

"I um…sorry," Jasper stammers. "I shouldn't have called you that."

I kiss him, admitting mid-kiss, "I like it, my pretty boy."

He bites my lip, drawing some blood that I lick away with a moan, telling him honestly, "And I'm open to all the pet names you want to call me."

"Ok…"Jasper murmurs before kissing me, licking away the blood still lingering on my lips. That causes my dick to throb, and I break the kiss with a groan.

"But now, pretty boy your mouth needs to do something else."

"Like what, baby?" Jasper taunts, smirking at me and showing his sexy dimples.

"Sucking my cock, pretty boy."

"Mmm…" Jasper moans, licking his plump lips. "I want to feel you explode in my mouth."

I shift to lie down next to him on my back. Jasper moves to kneel between my spread legs. I'm thankful he's got a double bed or it'd be super squishy.

He gives me no warning, taking my entire hard dick into his mouth. I grip his hair and pull him off.

"Go slow, pretty boy. I want to see my dick sliding between those lips."

He follows the request, just taking the tip in between his puffy lips. His tongue teases my slit and I let out a loud moan.

"Fuck, Jasp. Feels so good," I groan, once more grabbing his hair, this time to shove him down to take my dick deeper into his mouth.

He moans around it, licking over my length as he takes my dick in and out in a perfect rhythm. Again I grip his hair, holding him still as I start to throb in his mouth, my balls tightening with my impending release.

"Fuck, pretty boy, I'm gonna come so hard down your throat."

He moans as I hold him down, letting go and filling his mouth with come. He takes it all, swallowing with my dick still in his mouth.

"Fuck," I curse out, a final jolt hitting me as Jasper pulls off my dick. He sighs and I pull him to my side, kissing his forehead. There are so many words I want to say, but I stay silent as we both close our eyes, cuddling as we fall asleep.

CHAPTER TWENTY-NINE

Jasper

'm lying on my stomach, with my eyes fluttering closed in between the stages of sleep whilst my hard dick is rubbing against the mattress. I swear I can feel Reece behind me, the sensation of him dragging his erect dick between my arse cheeks teasing my pucker with the tip. He edges in, slightly and I clench around him, calling out, "Oh god, Reece! Fuck me harder!" I can't help but moan, thrusting against the mattress to edge closer to release. Groaning I roll over, pushing my hips up off the bed, my whole body trembling as I come.

My movement startles Reece, my eyes fully opening when he mumbles groggily, "Jasp?"

I glance at him from the corner of my eye, wondering for a moment how he's beside me and not at the foot of the bed. "Huh?" I mumble, holding back a yawn.

"Are you awake?" Reece asks, his eyes capturing mine in the dim lamplight.

I yawn then, mumbling, "Kinda."

Reece eyes me, puzzled as his eyebrows quirk upward. "Were you asleep?"

"Yeah, sorta. I was drifting off. Why?" I ask, feeling the sheets beneath me are wet with come.

"You were dreaming about us fucking and the bed was moving."

"I was?" I stammer, my cheeks flushing. He nods at me, a smirk teasing his lips that causes my stomach to flip.

"Ah...fuck. I can't believe it."

"What Jasp? Believe what? It was just a dream."

I shake my head at him, rolling onto my side to not have to face him when I confess. "I um...I have sexsomnia."

Reece grabs my side, forcing me to roll back over to face him. He's eyeing me incredulously.

"Seriously?" he gasps, still glaring at me like I'm a complete weirdo. I've never told anyone before about the condition I've been experiencing since early puberty. It comes out of nowhere most of the time and I also–unless someone points it out–I'm not even fully aware that it's happened.

"Yeah, I didn't want to tell you," I admit, looking away from Reece's gaze locked on mine. "It just happens sometimes and I slip in and out of sleep while I'm masturbating."

"Sounds like a wet dream," Reece observes.

I shake my head, once again glancing at him. My heart is pounding. "It's different to that. I'm not always fully asleep when it happens and I'm aware of what I'm doing. It's like a daze, a trance of sorts."

Reece nods but doesn't say anything in response, so I add, "But also sometimes afterwards, I don't even remember it happening unless someone tells me like you just did."

Again Reece gasps, smirking when he replies, "Well, it sounded hot, Jasper."

"It's hard to explain. I hope you don't think I'm some sex-crazed weirdo."

Reece scoffs. "You sex crazed?"

I nod but don't say a word. "Definitely not something I'd say to describe you, Jasp."

"Ok, um, good..." I stammer, my voice breaking.

Reece chuckles. "Do you want to fuck?" The question takes me aback, literally coming out of nowhere.

"I guess. But not right now," I respond, again yawning.

That causes Reece to laugh once more, and he taunts, "Go to sleep pretty boy," as he gives me a lingering kiss that causes every nerve ending in my body to spark. I want more with Reece, to actually feel him sliding inside me, to come with his dick buried in my arse. But I can't want that. Dreaming about it is one thing, a sin. But actually following through on the act, giving into that temptation is taking things to the next level, and committing the ultimate sin.

I don't verbalise my thoughts, instead, I roll over, facing away from Reece and snuggling under the covers, with Reece spooning me as we fall asleep. Even this, having him sleeping beside me in bed, knowing that we'll wake up in each other's arms–with morning wood, no doubt–is a sin enough. Reece surely must be the devil, because every moment we spend together is further cementing my place in hell.

CHAPTER THIRTY

REECE

As usual, I'd been summoned to my father's office by his bellowing voice filling the entranceway of our house. There's definitely no sneaking in or out of this house. Sighing, I reluctantly rap my knuckles on his office door. Normally I'd barge in but I can hear a hushed voice speaking to my father that has me hesitating. Despite the hushed tone, the voice is familiar and when my father lets me into his office I'm not surprised to see Alaric Exton standing there.

What is surprising is that he's in uniform, complete with his bulletproof vest and his gun holster.

He gives me a nod in greeting and I greet him with a hint of formality, "Hello, Chief Exton."

"Good day, Reece," he responds.

My father glares at me. "Enough with the pleasantries," he bites out, still glaring at me, now with more malice.

"This is not a pleasant visit then?" I ask, glancing between them both for an answer.

"No, Reece, it is not," Alaric voices.

"Is Malyk ok?" I ask, concerned for my best friend's welfare with his uncle being here.

"Yes, Malyk is as fine as my delinquent of a nephew can be. I'm here as a warning."

My father clears his throat. "You've been careless, son," my father berates.

"With what?"

Alaric steps into my personal space, which causes me to shrink back, stumbling a little towards the door.

"You involved Bartholomew in business you were told to keep private," he informs me.

I scoff, even though I'm shaking in my boots.

"Are you fucking serious? I couldn't have kept anything about that incident from Barth. He knew. It was his girlfriend that was assaulted."

"Yes, and we were aware of that, but you dealt with the accused in a manner that was far beyond what was needed and involved Bartholomew in the clean up. He didn't exactly do that discreetly," Alaric informs me, his tone accusatory and stern.

Again I scoff, frustrated with my cousin for being sloppy.

"So, go tell Barth that, and give him a talking to instead. I did what I always do, and that's to off Capullo scum."

Alaric frowns. "One day soon, if this involvement of others outside of our arrangement continues, dear boy I will not be able to turn a blind eye."

"You'd take your nephew's best friend away? Without a care for his well-being?"

"I would despise having to do so, but the choice would not be mine."

"Would I pay for all my crimes?"

"Yes, so please be more careful dear boy, and it will not come to that. I appreciate your efforts in keeping our streets free of those that will to cause harm to the greater good."

"Noted, Chief Exton. I'll be more careful," I reply, nodding and air quoting for emphasis. I turn to glare at my father. "Nothing to say, Father?"

"Nothing that you want to hear."

"Fine, then I'll be going," I announce turning towards the door. My father stops me though, tugging on my arm.

"Not so fast, son. I said you'd not want to hear what I have to say, however, you need to hear it."

Wrenching my arm free, I huff. Alaric nods at my father. "I'll be off Giovanni. Good day."

"Good day Alaric, and thank you for your support and discretion."

"Always for you, Giovanni."

Alaric leaves then, leaving me alone with my father. Once more I turn to leave, but my exit is halted by my father's booming voice, "Reece Mattheus Montserrat! Don't you dare leave before we speak."

Turning to face him—not moving closer—I smile, albeit a fake one, but still, it's a smile. He sees right through the facade I'm trying to put on.

"Do you have anything to admit to me, Reece?"

"About what?"

"Who you've been sneaking off to see at all hours of the night."

"You keeping tabs on me father? Got cameras in the dorms?"

He scoffs mockingly. "There are cameras, yes, but those are not concerned with your whereabouts."

"So you've got some fucker on my arse then?"

"Do not curse at me, Reece. And people have seen things. You've been associating with the enemy."

Fuck. My father's henchmen have seen me with Jasper or leaving his dorms. I'd been contemplating telling him—and my mother about Jasper—but that's not possible with this reaction. If he finds out I'm with Jasper, that we have done a helluva lot more than associate with each other I'll be cast out, denied my name. That might not be a bad thing, however, with that comes poverty as my father would cut my trust fund.

"Well, father, your henchmen must be mistaken. The only enemies I've associated with are the ones you've required me to eradicate."

"That best be so, Reece. You know the consequences of disobedience."

I nod, biting down on my lip so I don't scoff at his choice of words. Disobedience sounds as though I'm a child who misbehaved, not an adult capable of making my own decisions.

"Yes, father," I mumble. "May I go now?"

"You may be excused. And mind yourself in public. Eyes are everywhere, and I will find out about any miscreant behaviour."

I wait as he moves around to the other side of his desk, and sits in his foreboding chair. I can feel his seething gaze on my back as I go to leave. There's only one person I want to see right now, but I don't dare go to his dorms. I need to lay low on seeing Jasper for a while, even though it will kill me slowly.

CHAPTER THIRTY-ONE

Jasper

On break from uni, Nancy is over, and we're sitting on my bed. She's telling me about the new guy she's been seeing, but I'm not actually listening, spaced out instead, thinking about Reece. It's been weeks since I've seen him and almost just as long since we've texted. Stupidly, I miss him.

"Jasp, are you even listening?" Nancy asks rather loudly, causing me to mumble out a stunned 'huh' before biting down on my lip, admitting, "Sorry Nanc, no I was lost in my head."

"Thinking about him?" she questions me. I'm annoyed that I don't even need to hear his name to know exactly who she's referring to.

"Yeah, I know I shouldn't be thinking such salacious thoughts about my enemy. And I most certainly should not be committing sins of the flesh with him but I can't fight it anymore."

Nancy smiles widely at my admission. That unnerves me. "You're in love with him, aren't you?"

I shake my head. "One cannot love the one they're born to hate, Nancy."

She scoffs at me, shaking her head also. "That is a fallacy, Jasper. There is but a fine line between love and hate, and you've crossed it, my dear friend."

I sigh deeply, exhaling with my admittance, "I don't love him." Nancy frowns at me, her pout mirroring my own. "I cannot love him, and be the man my father wishes I be."

"You need to live and love the way your heart chooses. Do not let others, especially your parents choose your path."

Again I sigh, this time sliding across the bed to hug her. "I love you, Nancy. You're the greatest of friends."

"I love you too, Jasper," Nancy responds, her tone mellow. Our love is different, platonic.

"Why couldn't I love you like a man loves a woman?" I verbalise, it more as a statement than a question.

"Because that isn't your desire, Jasp. Your sexuality is not that way."

I laugh softly, divulging, "I don't know what my sexuality is." Nancy doesn't appear shocked by my confession, so I continue stumbling on my words,

"I…it has always confused me with how I feel about and how I'm attracted to others."

Nancy smiles at me once more. "Well, simple question…are you attracted to just guys, or both girls and guys?"

"It's not that simple Nanc. I don't honestly care about gender. It's the person for me, not their gender."

Nancy again smiles, this time giggling. "Jasp, my dearest, it sounds like you're pansexual."

I ponder the word in my head, testing it out. It feels right, so I respond to Nancy with a laugh, "Yeah, and by god if Father knew the sins my sexuality has caused me to commit."

Nancy shakes her head. "Jasper, you need to let go of the notion of sin. Go to confession and bare all, seek absolution and make peace with who you are."

"You make that seem so simple. I will be judged and cast out for being with the enemy, a man, not a woman."

"That may be so, but let me ask you this…" she pauses and I look at her expectantly. "Is being with Reece worth being cast out?"

I nod. There is no other response to that question. "Yes. He causes my heart to ignite and sets my entire body alight and we have not even copulated."

Nancy laughs. "You and your big words. Just say fucked, Jasper."

"Fucked," I say testing the word out on my tongue. "We haven't fucked."

"You want to be fucked?" Nancy questions, quirking her eyebrow up and laughing.

"Yeah, I want to be fucked by Reece Montserrat," I respond, both of us erupting into laughter together and falling back on the bed.

"Then go to confession and afterwards, let your man worship you, Jasper."

"Eww, Nancy."

She laughs again, standing up and heading out, calling out to me, "I'm going to go and get fucked myself."

"Too much information, Nanc!"

Once Nancy leaves, I quickly dress in some nicer clothes—three quarter jeans and a button down chambray shirt—that I roll the sleeves of up to my elbows. I slip on some loafers, grab my phone and head out to go to confession.

At the church, I get out of the car hesitantly after parking out front. The catholic church I grew up going to every Sunday until recently looks foreboding, causing apprehension to bubble in my stomach as I take each stone step up to the wooden double entrance doors. My heart is galloping in my chest. I'm so nervous just being in the church, let alone about to confess to a priest of the sins I've committed with Reece. I know they're sins of the flesh–and mind–but they've never felt like sinning. It's never felt like sinning with him.

Exhaling deeply, I shove my hands against the double doors and they easily swing open. The moment I step into the foyer I gasp for breath, my throat feels dry as though I've stepped into a place devoid of oxygen.

Swallowing hard I start to walk down the aisle of the church towards the altar and confessional boxes. There's not another soul around which doesn't do a thing to calm my nerves.

There is a priest in the confession box closest to the altar and I slip into the parishioner's side, sitting down on the ledge seat and exhaling a deep sigh.

His voice is deep, "Confess your sins dear child of God."

Again I exhale deeply, puffing my chest out as I let the words out, "I'm falling for the enemy."

The priest doesn't respond. I can hear his heavy breathing. I continue my confession, "I've let him violate my body and I've craved the pleasure. Wanted the sin of sex without population."

"Your sins have been heard dear child of God. And you have been absolved of all your sins upon your confession," the priest announces, softly exhaling before asking calmly, "Do you have any other worldly concerns for discussion?"

Once more I take in a deep breath, loudly verbalising with my exhale, "I'm going to let him fuck me."

I leave without letting the priest respond to that, shoving the door of the confessional box open I only hear his shocked gasp as I run out of the church with my chest heaving.

As I get in my car, I inhale gulps of air and text Reece.

Come to my house. 125 Mount Vemore Views Rd.

Why?

I want to sin with you.

Sinning sounds fun, What do you have in mind?

The ultimate sin.

I pocket my phone and start my car before driving home in haste, thinking about being with Reece completely.

CHAPTER THIRTY-TWO

Jasper

Despite my texting Reece hours ago–with my address–and the invitation of sex he hasn't turned up and I can't get in contact with him. I don't know how to feel about that fact. Does he not want to be with me? Did something happen with his family? So many questions are running through my mind.

Considering his radio silence, it's probably a stupid idea, but I can't sit here any longer and wait for him so I rush out to my car and head to the pub. It's the only place I can think of that he might be, tuning out the chaos of our shitty town.

Showing up at the pub I immediately want to leave. I've walked straight into something I shouldn't be a part of. Reece is in the middle of a job, holding a guy around the throat with him pinned against the wall whilst he seethes in his face. I shouldn't but I step closer to them. "Reece," I say raspy. He turns his head to glare at me, his grip loosening on the guy he's got pinned against the wall.

"Capullo, what the fuck are you doing here?" he seethes at me.

"You didn't come over. I was worried."

"I'm busy, dickhead."

"Um, yeah, I'll go…" I stammer, stepping away. Reece is staring at me, his hand shifting off his target. The guy whimpers, moving away from Reece.

Reece's gaze bounces between us, and he huffs.

"Don't you dare fucker!" he shouts at his hostage.

"What are you gonna do, arsehole?" the guy seethes at Reece. They're staring each other down and it's causing my heart to race. Time stands still, all of a sudden and the guy pulls out a gun, literally from nowhere. He points it at Reece, and I swear my heart stops. This stranger is about to kill Reece–the guy I shouldn't be in 'love' with–but honestly, I think I do love him. And that is just as scary to be facing as this scene playing out in front of me. I close my eyes, taking slow steps back until my back hits a car. My heart is still racing, and again jolts in my chest when a gunshot goes off, the sound near deafening but not as loud as my scream. It's broad daylight. anyone could have seen this shootout. I don't want to open my eyes, don't want to know if Reece has been shot. If he's dead my whole world will shatter. Life won't be worth living without Reece in it.

I'm sobbing now, tears leaking out of my still tightly shut eyes when I feel a tight grip on my arm. I'm shoved aside by the car door behind me opening and flutter my eyes open to find Reece shoving me into his car. I go willingly, desperate to get away from this situation before someone is dead. Reece rushes around the bonnet, getting into the driver's seat and we race off, heading to the Capullo side of the city.

"Reece…what…happened?" I stammer, glancing in the rear window to see cars spilling out of every street corner, following us.

"Job gone wrong, and now we're being followed by Capullo gang members." His tone is scathing when he says 'Capullo'. It's a warning, an accusatory one as though he's implying it's my fault.

"I didn't do this, Reece."

"Didn't say you did, but it's a little uncanny, Capullo," he seethes, speeding up as the cars behind give chase. They sped up behind us, one colliding in warning with the back bumper. Reece speeds off more, and I glance into the door mirrors to see a passenger from the car directly behind us leaning out the window with his gun cocked. He shoots at the car, the bullet clanging against the metal. I sink down into my seat, petrified that the bullets he's still firing towards Reece's car are going to impact us and I'll die beside Reece. That can't happen, and if these guys giving chase are really on my side they'll back off if we head down Mount Vemore Views Road. Every Capullo–or acquaintance of our family–knows anyone who heads down 'our' road, to the top of the hill is welcome. They're no enemy.

Reece slows the car down a little, glancing over at me, laughing.

"You right, Jasp?"

"No, we're being shot at, Reece."

"Nothing I can do about it."

"Yeah, there is," I mumble. He gives me a confused look, quirking his eyebrow up.

"Care to share?"

I nod, sitting up in the seat a little. "Take the turn up ahead onto Mount Vemore Views road, and drive all the way to end to the iron gates on the hill."

"Where are you leading me to? Sounds like another cemetery."

"It's my house," I tell him, reaching over the console to grip his thigh. "And whoever is chasing us won't dare follow."

He nods, not replying but he takes my hand with his and yanks the steering wheel tightly to careen around the bend onto my street. This might be a bad idea, but I don't think there's any other option.

CHAPTER THIRTY-THREE

REECE

Taking the turn onto Mount Vemore View Road, just as Jasper said we're no longer being followed. I'm still clutching Jasper's hand in mine with our fingers laced together. His breathing is returning to normal and I glance across at him as I drive up the hill. Jasper could've gotten hurt because I fucked up and didn't think to send him a fucking message when he was expecting my presence at his house. I inadvertently involved Jasper in a job, and I'm surely going to suffer a consequence for that stupidity. This feud is killing me. I've gotta find a way to sort it out. My father's words about my fraternising with the enemy come to mind as I get to the top of the hill, stopping in front of the iron gates of Jasper's family mansion. I think maybe I need to be honest, to talk to my father openly and admit the truth. It'll probably be a complete disaster but I can't continue living in the shadows with Jasper. He deserves more than that.

Jasper taps something on his phone, and the gates swing open in front of the car.

"Drive in, and head to the left. You can park under the weeping willow tree."

I nod, following his directions and spotting the willow tree easily. I pull up the car, turn the ignition off, and sigh deeply. Jasper squeezes my hand again.

"Sorry about your car," he says, giving me a shy smile.

"You don't have to be sorry about that, Jasp. It fucking sucks, but at least I'm not dead."

He smiles wider. "I'm glad you're not dead too."

Engaging the door release button I don't respond to that statement. It hits me in the feels too much for right now, when we're sitting in my beat up car.

He slides out and I follow, locking the car before I walk to his side. Once more he takes my hand, tightly gripping it as he drags me towards the front door.

He taps a key code into the keypad lock and the doors open to let us inside. My eyes boggle at the grand staircase in front of us, at the paintings on the wall—portraits of his family and landscapes—that are stunningly beautiful. I want to ask if he painted them, but he's already dragging me down a narrow hallway on the lefthand side of the stairs.

"Come on, my room is this way," he coaxes, stretching out his arm to pull me along faster.

I laugh. "Someone's keen for some dick."

"Shh, I don't know if my parents are home."

At the end of the hallway, he pushes open a set of double doors, yanking me inside his bedroom. It's practically its own fucking mansion, with a giant tv mounted on the wall, a floor to ceiling window with a sheer curtain and a king size cast iron bed in the middle.

"Fuck, Jasp. Your room is a fucking palace."

"Ah yeah, it's my happy place," he admits, glancing around at his space. He drops my hand, flicking a lock on the doors behind me.

I look around his room more, noticing the easel, pile of canvases—with unfinished paintings—and paint supplies.

He sits down on the edge of his bed and following I ask him, "Are the paintings in the hallway yours?"

He shakes his head. "No, they were done by my grandfather. He taught me all he knew about art."

"That's pretty special. I'm sorry you lost him at the hand of a Montserrat."

"It's not your fault, Ree. It's not like you killed him."

"Yeah I know, Jasper. Doesn't make me feel any less guilty for the harm and heartbreak my family has caused yours."

He bites down on his lip, glaring at me as though he's lost for words. His gaze then drops to the bed, but he can't hide the tears that are slipping down his cheeks.

"Jasp? You ok?"

He shakes his head, mumbling, "Mmm. No. You. We…"

"We what?" I ask, grabbing his hand and squeezing it. The gesture causes his gaze to lift and meet mine.

"We could have died today, and never had the chance to be together completely," he sniffs.

Again his words hit me right in the damn feels. Whether I like it or not I've got feelings for Jasper.

"You saying you want to be fucked Jasper? Just in case tomorrow never comes?"

"Tomorrow is only a promise, not a guarantee," he says, shifting so our thighs brush.

The fleeting touch sends a jolt through my body.

"Stop talking then, Capullo and kiss me," I taunt, grabbing the front of his chambray shirt and yanking him closer so our lips brush. He whimpers softly as I take his lips in a kiss that sets my whole body alight with longing. Fuck I've missed him.

How did I ever think I could stay away from him? Being with Jasper gives me life.

Breaking the kiss, I tug on the front of his shirt.

"Take it off, Jasper," I request, smirking at him suggestively. He slowly unbuttons his shirt, letting it fall off his arms to the bed. With a hand against his chest, I push him down onto the bed, again kissing him. His hips buck up to meet mine, the friction causing our dicks to harden in our jeans.

His hands slide up under my t-shirt, and I hiss against his lips at the touch which sends a shiver through me.

Gasping I break the kiss, murmuring, "Fuck, your hands on my body feel incredible, Jasp."

He bites his lip, bucking his hips up again. "Mmm, I..." he mumbles through his teeth.

"What Jasper? Tell me what you want."

"Touch me."

"You asking? Or telling?" I sass, smirking at him.

"Telling," he admits with a smile.

"You're a brat, Capullo," I jeer, reaching down to undo the fly of his jeans.

I make quick work of tugging his dark jeans down his legs, throwing them on the floor before I lean down, kissing his hardening dick over the fabric of his white boxers. They colour with a wet spot, his dick leaking precum from my lips on his length.

"More, please, Reece, more," he begs, shivering.

I flip his dick out of his boxers, and lick it from his groin to the tip, teasing the slit with my tongue to lap up the precum.

"Oh god, Reece please...please," he again begs, writhing around on the bed as though I'm giving him the greatest pleasure. No one I've been with before Jasper has ever been so responsive in bed, and that turns me the fuck on.

He also causes my selfishness to wane. I want nothing more than to give Jasper pleasure, without needing him to give back the same. He can make me come without a touch, so it's no harm. Having his mouth on my dick feels incredible, yes, but I don't need to feel that to feel mind numbing pleasure with him.

Yanking his boxers off, I discard them to the floor before spreading his legs wide as I take his dick into my mouth. He moans loudly, his eagerness turning me on as I pull off and shift back on the bed to strip out of my clothes. Jasper watches me the entire time as I slowly strip, pouting. It's damn sexy.

And I tease him, "You horny Jasp?"

"Yes, please. Need you," he rasps, eyeing my hard dick. With my hands on his thighs, I part them more and kneel between his legs, bending down to lick his pucker. He screams out, "Fuck!" And I reach up to cover his mouth, delving my tongue into his arse, whilst stifling his moans of pleasure with my hand over his mouth. I'm going to have him begging for my cock inside him. Begging for me to make him mine. Because that's who he is. Jasper Capullo is mine.

CHAPTER THIRTY-FOUR

Jasper

Reece is tonguing my arse, gripping my thighs to hold me still. My dick is throbbing, leaking precum and I'm desperate to come, for more. Moaning against the hand Reece has over my mouth, I lick his palm and he removes his hand, pulling back to look up at me.

His smirk is beguiling. "You want me to stop, Jasp?" he questions me, winking.

"No, I want you to fuck me."

He laughs at my request, and I pout. "Don't you want to?"

"Don't be dense, Capullo. Of course I want to, but you're not ready."

I scoff, letting out an exasperated huff of annoyance. "I am ready." I know I sound like a petulant child. I want him. I want everything with him.

CAZ MAY

Again Reece laughs. "Relax, Jasp. I don't mean it that way, I just need to prep you, until you're begging me to fuck you."

I don't get to respond as he leans over to kiss me, one hand cupping my jaw, the other sliding down between my spread legs to brush a digit against my pucker. Still kissing me, he slips one finger in, slowly fucking me with it. It causes me to moan against his mouth and break the kiss.

"More, Reece, more," I beg, and he chuckles as he slides another finger inside my hole, curling it up to tease my prostate. His touch against that spot is amazing. But I need more than his fingers inside me, and he did say he wants me begging him to fuck me.

"Reece!" I practically scream out, lifting my head off the pillow to glare at him. He stills his fingers inside me. "Fuck me now!"

He shakes his head, his signature wicked smirk on his face. "Not until you suck my cock, Jasper," he taunts.

I pout at him, lifting my head and folding my arms across my chest. "I just want you to fuck me," I plead.

"Suck my cock, Jasper," he demands, his voice with a cheeky lilt. He shifts then, yanking my arms apart and sliding up over my torso until his semi hard dick is in my face, the tip touching my lips.

Involuntarily, I swipe my tongue across my lips, teasing the tip of his dick which causes him to moan loudly and grip the bedhead as he shifts forward to push his dick between my lips.

I swirl my tongue over his length as he fucks my mouth, panting, "God, Jasper, fuck!"

I grip his hips, and he slips out of my mouth, giving me a confused look. "Please, Reece, I need you inside me." He reaches behind him to grab my hard dick, stroking it a few times before asking, "Do you have lube? Condoms?"

"Um, I have lube, but not condoms," I respond, blushing and shaking my head.

"Fuck," he curses under his breath, moving off me and standing by the end of the bed to pull off the rest of his clothes.

I take his hand and he looks straight at me worriedly. "Is that a problem?"

He sighs, and with a gentle tug, he sits on the edge of the bed at my feet.

"Well, yeah, maybe," he admits. "I haven't been with anyone else since I've been with you, but last time I was tested it wasn't a negative result."

"Oh, so you got treated though?"

"Yeah, but I didn't go for my follow-up test."

Again, I take his hand, sitting up and kissing him softly. "I trust you, Reece," I tell him. "If anything happens as a result we'll deal with it together."

He kisses me, harder and deeper, his tongue dancing with mine and he gently bites my lip, drawing a hint of blood which he licks away with his tongue. "Thanks, Jasper. I don't deserve you."

I laugh, replying, "Yeah you do, arsehole." He gives me another kiss, before pulling back and asking, "Where's the lube?"

"Top drawer," I reply, nodding towards my bedside drawers. He stands and scoots to the other side of the bed to grab it. He crawls across the bed towards me, flicking open the top of the tube and squeezing some of the lube onto his finger.

"Spread your legs, pretty boy."

I obey quickly, opening my legs wide. He looks straight into my eyes, as he rubs the lube over my pucker, his finger slipping inside to again fuck me with it.

"You ready, Jasper?" he asks, his voice soft. My heart is pounding in my chest. I can't believe this is happening, but I've never been more sure of anything in my life.

"Yes," I rasp. "I'm ready Reece. Fuck me."

He shifts on the bed, so he's between my legs and lines himself up with the tip of his dick against my pucker. I gasp, inhaling a breath I don't exhale.

"Jasp, relax, baby," he coaxes, pressing against my body and leaning down to sweep the hair out of my eyes before giving me a soft kiss.

"You called me baby," I mumble.

"Yeah, you going to relax for me?"

I sigh, exhaling the breath as he again kisses me, pushing further inside me, his tip breaching the ring of muscle. I gasp against his lips. "Fuck, Reece."

He releases my lips, cupping my cheeks. "You ok? Want more?"

"Yes, more, please," I beg, my heart racing. It hurts, like really hurts. I bite down on my lip as he shoves deeper inside me, stilling his body when his pelvis hits mine.

Jolts of pain are shooting through every nerve in my body. Is this so much of a sin that I'm cursed for it to hurt?

"Fuck, it hurts," I hiss.

"I said relax, Capullo."

I sigh, grabbing his cheeks and kissing him, biting his lips so he feels the pain. He starts to rock in and out, and slowly the pain dissipates turning to blinding pleasure that has me ripping our lips apart, and screaming, "Fuck!"

Reece stills his thrusts. "Still hurt?"

"No, it feels so good," I admit. "Fuck me harder, Reece."

He stretches his body up, and I admire his tattoos, lifting my head a little to watch his dick penetrating my arse as he drives into my hole harder, faster and more punishing.

"Oh, god, Reece, baby, there, fuck!" I call out, not giving a shit that my voice can probably be heard at the bottom of the hill. It feels too good to care.

"You like me fucking your tight arse, Jasper?"

"Yes, yes, more!" I groan, yanking him down by a fist around his neck to kiss him. I fuck his mouth with my tongue whilst he fucks my arse as though he owns me, and he does. I'm his. My heart, my body, my entire being belongs to my enemy, to Reece Montserrat. I could never have given myself to another.

He pulls all the way out and pulls me into his lap as he sits down. I go willingly, following his lead because I'm putty for him. I'd do anything he asked me right now.

He grabs the lube again, palming his dick to cover it more.

Leaning in he whispers in my ear, "Ride me, pretty boy."

I wrap my legs around his back, shifting more so I'm in his lap. He pushes his hips up, easily sliding inside me and I groan. This angle makes me feel so full. And so incredible.

"Jasper," Reece rasps against the shell of my ear. "I said ride my cock."

I moan, panting as I start to bounce up and down on his dick inside my arse.

"It…it feels…so good," I rasp, stilling my rocking hips as Reece bites my neck, trailing hickeys down to my collarbone. He grips my jaw, kissing me fiercely as I rock on his dick.

"Take it all, Jasper."

"Ah…ah..fuck…" I groan. "There, there."

Reece thrusts up into me as I bare down, and it hits that spot. Nothing could feel better than this. I glance into my lap, noticing my dick bobbing between us and grab it to stroke myself a little.

"Hands off your dick, baby."

I pout, and he kisses me when I let go of my dick. "Why?" I question.

"Because you're going to come hands free with my cock buried in your arse, Jasper."

"Oh god, yes," I pant as he pushes up into me again.

He thrusts in a few more times, his dick starting to throb inside me, indicating that he's close.

"Are you coming?" I ask, my cheeks colouring.

Moaning, he pants, "Yes, Jasper, fuck!"

I roll my hips, squeezing his dick with my channel and letting go, spilling come all over his stomach.

"Fuck Jasper!" he moans, his dick pulsing inside my arse, filling me with his come.

He kisses me, and I smile against his lips.

"That was amazing, Reece," I admit, as his softening dick falls from inside me and I lay down on my back.

He lies down next to me, and pulls me into his arms, cuddling me close. There are no more words to exchange, nothing that could describe the pleasure we just shared.

I turn my head to face him and kiss him deeply. With the kiss, I'm hoping all the feelings he invokes in me are felt by him. I'm his. I belong to Reece Montserrat, and soon I'm going to tell him and the world that he's no longer my enemy. He never really was, and it was never—and never will be—sinning with him.

CHAPTER THIRTY-FIVE

REECE

Opening my eyes, I fling my arms out realising I'm not in my bed, but still in Jasper's bed after we slept together last night. Hands down it was the best sex of my life, how responsive he was and how hard we both came, multiple times until the early hours of the morning. He's not next to me now, the bed cold as though he's been gone for some time. I'm kinda disappointed he's skipped out and isn't still in my arms, as I'd welcome some morning fucking. I have a raging hard on and tug on my dick a few times to calm it down before sliding out of the bed and tugging on my t-shirt, boxers and jeans from the floor.

Heading to the bedroom door, I can hear music playing…from a piano. It's reverberating off every wall and is melodic and soothing. I sneak out into the hallway, following the sound to a room on the other side of the grand staircase with expansive double ornate doors. This house is a damn palace. My family is rich, but our house is modern opulence—the original mansion having burnt down when I was only a baby as part of the fucked up feud of our families—whereas Jasper's family home is their original mansion, and it's spectacular.

I push open the doors, finding Jasper playing a baby grand piano in the middle of the room. He's surrounded by a wall-to-wall ceiling-high library complete with one of those sick sliding ladders. I'm no bookworm, but even I can't but not love this space, partly because I know Jasper would love it.

Jasper stops playing—sensing my presence in the room as I saunter closer—and he looks at me coming into the room.

I chuckle softly, stepping up behind him. "Don't stop on my account, Jasp."

"You can't be in here, Reece," he responds, biting down on his lip nervously. That gesture always causes my dick to stir, and now is no exception.

"Why? No one's here," I taunt. "And I woke up in bed without you."

He gives me a shy smile. "Sorry, I needed to clear my head after last night."

I nod. "No need to apologise." Clearly, having sex with Jasper has turned me into a sap. Showing feelings is not something I'd do before him.

I sit on the edge of the piano stool, next to him.

"Play me something," I whisper into his ear. He shivers and I kiss his cheek, then murmur, "Your favourite."

Jasper starts playing, something classical that sounds familiar. I'm mesmerised watching his fingers sliding across the keys effortlessly. I join in, pressing random keys. Jasper stops and laughs, "You're messing up the song, Ree."

"Just putting my spin on it. What song is it anyway?"

"Sounds like your demon Raven dying with your added parts," Jasper responds laughing, adding with a smirk, "It was Moonlight Sonata by Beethoven."

"Oh right," I answer, nodding, before giving him a cheeky death glare. "Rave is not a demon. He just doesn't like people who don't like him."

Jasper giggles, shaking his head. "You can't blame me for my dislike of your cat, Ree. He hissed at me the first time I met him." I love him calling me Ree—especially after last night—it feels intimate.

"I know. He's just protective of his daddy is all."

"Eww, Reece," Jasper says, screwing his face up in disgust. "Don't ever refer to yourself as daddy around me."

I laugh, poking him playfully in the ribs as I tease him, "You don't want to call me daddy whilst I fuck your brains out?"

"Only if you never want to fuck me again," he scoffs.

"Well, I guess I'll be calling you daddy then," I jeer sarcastically.

Jasper laughs and I cup his jaw to turn his face to mine, kissing him. He's reluctant to kiss me back. "Kidding, Jasp. Fucking you last night was the best damn fuck of my life."

He smiles at me and then responds, "Likewise, Ree. I...ah...I...lo..." I cut him off with another kiss. There's no way in hell I'm going to let him say those three words first.

I deepen the kiss a moment, causing him to moan and kiss me back, desperately. If I was doubting what he was going to say before I'm certainly not now. Jasper Capullo is in love with me, and fuck me dead I love him right back.

I break the kiss, my forehead against his as I murmur, "I love you, Jasper Capullo. I absolutely fucking love you."

Jasper gasps, kissing me again, stealing the air from my lungs and any other declaration of the love I feel for him.

Against my lips, he whispers, "I love you, Reece Montserrat." I break the kiss with a gasp. I knew he felt the same, but hearing it fall from his beautiful lips causes my heart to race. I give him more kisses, and he murmurs softly, pulling back to look directly into my eyes, telling me, "And I'll deny my name to be with you."

I nod, affirming his words before sealing them against his pouty lips with a kiss.

"So would I. You'd no longer be a Capullo and I no longer a Montserrat."

Jasper kisses me again, a possessive kiss that has us both moaning and our dicks hardening in our pants. It's hot and frantic and killing me slowly until Jasper pulls back with a laugh.

"What are you thinking, love?" I ask, not even giving a shit at the caring term of endearment that escaped my mouth. He's not fazed by it, asking abruptly, "Have you ever fucked somewhere you shouldn't have?"

"You mean somewhere other than your bed?" I jeer at him tickling his side.

"Yeah," he stammers between his giggling.

Stopping my tickling, I admit, "I fucked a guy in my car once."

"Hmm," he murmurs, pondering the logistics. "Sounds awkward."

"Totally was. Have you?" I question, quirking my eyebrow.

Jasper blushes, confessing with a mumbled, "Last night was my first time."

"You're shitting me? I took your virginity?" I blurt out, shocked but at the same time I'm not surprised in the least.

"Yeah, I thought you knew that."

"I didn't. I kinda assumed but then thought it couldn't be possible."

His mouth falls open as though he's going to say something, but nothing comes out and he gulps.

"I'm sorry if I hurt you."

"You didn't. I ah…want you to fuck me again, right here, right now," he declares in a demanding tone that causes my dick to throb. Bratty Jasper is my favourite.

"You sure you aren't too sore?" I ask, shocking myself at how caring I'm being. In the past I couldn't have given a flying fuck if a guy was red raw after I'd fucked him, I'd go for round two without a care even if I caused him pain. But I can't do that to Jasper. If he's hurting I'll kiss him, and make him come with my mouth instead. I'm so cock whipped by my enemy, but he's not my enemy anymore, he's my everything. My greatest love from my greatest hate.

Jasper shakes his head. "No, fuck me now right here on the piano."

I groan, sliding off the stool and dropping to my knees. Gripping Jasper's hips I turn him around. He gasps but doesn't protest, shifting easily until his back hits the keys, causing the sound of the pressed keys to fill the room.

CHAPTER THIRTY-SIX

Jasper

The sound of my back hitting the piano keys fills the room. Reece is standing in front of me, with a wickedly sexy smirk as he pulls down my pj pants, yanking them off when they reach my knees.

"Reece, please," I pant, licking my lips as I stare back at him. Still smirking he drops to his knees, gripping my already hard dick in his hand. The tip is leaking precum and he slides his thumb over the slit to coat my dick with it.

I lean back, gripping the edge of the keys then as Reece takes my dick into his mouth, not at all slowly. He's got my dick in his mouth completely and he's swirling his tongue over every inch. He grips my dick with one hand, taking my dick in and out of his lips to suck me. The sounds escaping his mouth as he devours my dick like it's his favourite meal have me so on edge. I lean back further, gripping the keys harder and playing random notes.

"God, Reece!" I bellow, causing him to speed up his rhythm to the point it's punishing. "Feels so good," I pant, biting down on my lip for a moment. "Fuck, please, fuck me!" I scream out, my words raspy from the increasing pleasure pulsing through my body.

He pulls off, and smirks at me, taunting, "Beg me, pretty boy. Beg for me to fuck your tight hole."

He grabs my dick, squeezing the tip, his eyes locked on mine and daring me to challenge him.

"Fuck me now Reece. I need you to fuck me," I beg, not able to hide my desire for him.

Reece picks me up, with a strong grip on my hips and puts me down on the edge of the piano top, causing the lid to close a little, slipping down a couple of notches. The piano groans with the weight on it, but I honestly couldn't care less. Wouldn't even care if we broke it.

Looking right at Reece as he steps in between my legs I verbalise, "I love it when you manhandle me, Ree."

He groans then, loud and gruff and possessive. "I love you all spread out and ready for me, Jasp," he tells me, spreading my legs wider so I'm exposed to him.

Again he kneels down, this time to lave his tongue over my pucker.

"Oh," I gasp. "Feels so good, Ree."

CAZ MAY

He pushes his tongue inside, breaching the tight ring of muscle, soothing the soreness from last night. Pulling back, he then spits on my pucker, slipping a finger in to lube me up. He yanks his pants down and his fully hard dick is right there, at the perfect angle to slide right inside my hole.

"You want me to fuck you, pretty boy?" Reece asks, grabbing my waist.

"Yes, baby, fuck me," I respond.

Reece doesn't say a word as he slips inside my lubed hole, and he barely gives me a moment to adjust to having him fill me before he's thrusting hard, hitting my prostate with the tip of his dick.

"Fuck, Reece, fuck!" I call out grabbing the lid of the piano to hold onto, causing it's hinges to groan with every thrust. It's a quick, hard fuck and it's not long until we're both coming. I don't even touch my dick, and I spill come all over my stomach. Reece pulls out, moaning when he sees the mess I've made on myself. Leaning down he licks the come from my skin, laving his tongue over my stomach. It feels tickly, and I sit up, yanking him up by his hair to kiss him. I can taste myself on his tongue, and moan into his mouth, "Mmm, I can taste my come on your tongue, Ree."

He breaks the kiss, pecking the side of my lips. "I love…"Reece says, his words getting cut short by the doors careening open. A bellowing voice fills the room, "Jasper!"

I shove Reece aside and he yanks up his pants, not daring to turn around to see who has entered the room, but I'd know his voice anywhere and I'm deeply ashamed he's caught me with my pants down, after just coming.

I clamber off the piano, covering my dick with my hands awkwardly as shuffle around the piano to get my pants. Tugging them on, I stumble across to the other side of the piano where Reece has now turned towards the intruder.

"Montserrat," Tidus seethes, glaring at Reece as though he's about to strike him.

"Tidus," Reece responds, the same malice in his voice that causes my insides to flip, as it almost seems possessive over me.

"What are you doing here with my cousin?" Tidus questions, his jaw tight.

Reece sniggers. "Fucking him, until you barged in like a bull."

"You would never."

Again Reece sniggers, smirking when he jibs, "Already did, twice last night and just now."

Tidus lunges at Reece, about to throw a punch at him but I slide across the floor, stepping in between them to stop him.

"Cousin," Tidus warns, staring at me. "Did you consent to this?"

"Yes, I did consent, cousin. I'm in love with him."

"Pfft, love," Tidus scoffs. "In love with a Montserrat, cousin. That's a death wish."

"Then so be it," I reply, nodding, and then looking at Reece, and pulling him against my side. "I would rather die than not be with Reece."

"You do not know what you're saying, cousin," Tidus says, lunging at Reece again. He shifts out my hold on him, and rushes towards the door. Tidus chases him out the door, before stalking towards me.

The look in his eyes is causing my heart to race–and not in a good way–and I stumble backwards until I hit the piano. It digs into my back but I don't dare move.

"So you're gay, cousin?" he asks, a hint of anger in his voice.

"No," I reply, shaking my head, not able to meet my cousin's intense stare. "I'm pansexual."

"What the fuck does that mean?"

"It doesn't matter, Tidus. All that matters is I'm in love with Reece."

"Yeah it does fucking matter. You're in love with a Montserrat."

"Please don't tell father. I'm not ready to tell him yet."

"I'm not telling uncle that you're gay. He won't fucking believe it."

"Thank you, now please leave me be. And send Reece back in if he's still here."

Tidus leaves and I sit back down at the piano, to continue playing the song I played for Reece. He doesn't come back in, so I finish playing and head to my room to finish packing to head back to the dorms.

CHAPTER THIRTY-SEVEN

REECE

After leaving Jasper's I speed straight to my parents house. I don't know if I'm ready for this needed conversation. But I'm in love with Jasper and over this family fucking feud that's keeping us hiding in the shadows.

With Jasper's cousin now knowing we're together, his family will surely know soon. And I'm worried for him, but I need to do this. I need to man up and tell my father I've fallen for the enemy.

Arriving at my parents' house I barge in, straight into my fathers office by crashing through the double doors like a bull. My heart is racing with nervousness and when my father glances up at me I stumble backwards, almost retreating. But I need to do this. I have to do this.

"Yes, Reece?" my father questions, his voice stern.

"I need to tell you something father."

"Then tell me, no point beating around the bush."

I sigh, inhaling a deep breath as I step closer to his foreboding desk. I grip the mahogany with my palms. "I've been seeing someone, and you won't like who."

"Cut the bullshit, Reece. You think I'm stupid and can't see through your words."

"I never said you were stupid, father. But this isn't easy for me to admit to you."

He stands from his chair, clenching his fists tightly. He's seething.

"Is this person male?"

"Yes, it's...J..." I gulp, my loves name caught on the tip of my tongue with my father's scathing glare.

"Out with it, Reece," he demands, his jaw ticking.

"It's Jasper Capullo."

"Our sworn enemies son?" Dad questions, his voice raising an octave so it sounds more like a statement than a question.

"Your enemy, not mine," I respond, inhaling some deep breaths to attempt to calm my racing heart. The look in my father's eyes is hatred. I can feel it filling the room. He rounds the desk, still clenching his fists as he stalks towards me. He's raging, and I'm starting to panic. He's a callous man, and I know his fists can bring me a world of pain if I don't obey him, or he doesn't like my choices.

"Our enemies are one and the same, Reece. And your actions are traitorous towards our lineage."

My stomach is in knots, but I have to tell him. I have to speak my truth.

"I'm in love with him, father."

"How dare you admit such heinous words to me," my father seethes, unballing his fists and lunging towards me. I should move away, to avoid his incoming hit. But I don't move even an inch. My breathing is heavy, my heart aching because I'm regretting even bringing it up now. My father raises his fist and I close my eyes, anticipating causing my heart to race even more.

He strikes me then, his fist slamming into my nose causing blood to gush out and down my face. It hurts. Really hurts and tears sting my eyes. Words of apology are caught on the tip of my tongue, but I don't want to apologise for loving Jasper. I shouldn't have to. Loving someone needs no apology, not to my father or anyone. I don't react, don't say another word, instead I leave. When I'm out the door I let the tears fall, realising that it's gonna be harder than I thought to be open with my feelings for Jasper. It seems as though my father to not going to accept Jasper, and that breaks my heart.

I don't want to be a Montserrat if I can't be with Jasper. Our last names are not who we are, and I will deny mine to be with him. I'm not sure if he's back in the dorms, but I get back in my car to head there anyway. At least in the confines of Jasper's dorm room we can be together freely, without anyone barging in to forbid us from expressing our love for each other.

CHAPTER THIRTY-EIGHT

Jasper

I've barely been back in the dorms for an hour when there's a tentative knock on the door. I don't want to answer it, to face anyone. My head is racing with thoughts of Reece, and how incredible it was to be with him completely but I'm petrified of my father finding out that I've not only been with a guy but my enemy.

Quickly, I tug on some grey sweats and stumble to the door. Opening it my heart plummets. Reece is standing in the hallway, his face bloody and streaked with tears. I grab his hand and pull him into my room, slamming the door behind him.

"What happened, baby? Who did this to you?"

He shakes his hand away, crossing the small space to sit on the edge of my bed.

"Reece, who did this to you?"

I'm feeling protective. Seeing Reece hurt, and in pain stabs at my heart. I can feel his pain as though it's my own.

Sitting down next to him, I take his hands again. "Reece, please baby," I plead, reaching one hand up to cup his jaw and turn his gaze to mine.

Reece exhales a deep sigh. "My father."

"Why?"

"Because I told him about you."

"You what?"

"I told him I love you, Jasper and he hit me for it. Cursed you out for being the enemy."

"You're not my enemy, Reece. I love you and you can't love the enemy."

"I know, but I regret telling him now. This feud is not ours, but it's still a threat to keep us from loving one another."

"Then we end it, Ree. We find out why this feud is still keeping our families at arm's length."

He sighs again. "I don't think it's that simple. Our love isn't going to end a generational feud, Jasp."

"It may not, but I for one cannot stand to see you hurt for no fault of your own."

"I don't know what we can do though, Jasper. My father keeps many a secret from me."

I lean forward and kiss his lips softly, drawing a gasp out. "Leave it to me. I will dig deeper and find out the truth, even if it kills me."

"I hope that is not the outcome, Jasp. I'd kill anyone for you, though," he promises me, kissing me again and pushing me down on the bed so he's straddling my hips.

"I love you, Reece," I say, stretching up to kiss him and licking the blood from his philtrum, causing him to moan.

"God, fuck, Jasper. You doing that turns me on so much. I love you so fucking much."

"Yeah, I wanna make you moan, Ree. Even when we're naked, skin on skin, I want you closer."

Reece groans, lifting his t-shirt over his head. He grips the waistband of my sweats, tugging on them to expose me.

"Get these off, now, pretty boy," he demands, licking his lips as he watches me shimmy them off. He helps by tugging them over my knees and down my calves before throwing them aside. His gaze roams my nakedness, causing my already hard dick to throb and slap against my stomach.

"Fuck, you're so beautiful, Jasper."

I moan, grabbing the front of his t-shirt to pull him down to the point I can nearly kiss him. "So are you, Ree. Now take your clothes off so I can see how beautiful you are, and your glorious tattoos."

Reece groans in response, kissing me hard and taking my breath away. Beneath his sweats that are rubbing against my skin, I can feel his dick hardening. I break the kiss and pout, huffing, "I said get naked, Reece."

He laughs, sitting up and smirking at me. "And why should I do that, pretty boy?"

"So you can fuck me, baby," I respond, my voice raspy, my gaze finding the bulge in his sweats.

"You make me so hard, Jasp. And I could never deny you when you ask me to fuck you."

I don't reply, just bite my lip as I watch Reece strip down to his Calvin Klein boxers. Reaching out, I palm his dick, causing him to groan as I slip my hand inside as he leans down to kiss me again. His kiss is wild, and frantic, and causes him to shudder as I tug off his boxers. My hand is covered in his precum, and tearing my mouth from his I observe him as I slide my hand between my legs to lube myself up. My hips buck up from the touch, but my own fingers don't feel near as good as his do.

"Fuck, Capullo. You touching yourself is so damn hot," Reece remarks, smirking and licking his lips. He drops his hand to mine, and guides me to finger fuck myself.

It's weirdly erotic, and has me moaning and panting. "Please Reece, I want you to fuck me now."

Reece laughs. "Someone's keen."

"For you, yes," I reply, pulling his hand away. He shifts so his dick is right ay my pucker, the tip just brushing the ring of muscle.

"You're my beautiful, dirty boy, Capullo," Reece rasps, slipping his dick inside my hole. "I want you to ride my cock."

He pulls out, and immediately I feel the loss. He shifts back on my bed, closer to the end near the window, and I follow sitting in his lap and kissing him.

"I love you, Reece," I moan against his mouth, shifting so I can wrap my legs around his back.

I push myself down, taking his dick inside my hole slowly, inch by inch. It's beyond amazing, sending shivers through my entire body.

"Fuck," I groan, tipping my head back as I start to bounce up and down on his dick. "Feels so good, baby."

"Yeah, pretty boy. Ride my cock," Reece rasps, stealing my lips in a kiss that's all tongue and lip biting, a dance that matches the deep thrusts of his hip–and his dick–inside me as I bear down until I'm taking every inch of him deep inside me. His tip grazes my prostate and I groan into his mouth, breaking the kiss with a loud gasp. "Fuck, Reece, fuck!"

His eyes light up and he stares right into my gaze locked on his. "You like riding my dick, pretty boy?"

"Yes, I love it," I gasp, kissing him again softly. "I love you."

He gives me another kiss, again stealing my breath. "I love you more, Jasper," he responds, causing my heart to race, because the conviction in his words that he loves me more than I love him is beyond incomprehensible, not at all possible. I love him more than words can truly say.

"And you're going to come for me, so hard you'll be seeing fucking stars, baby."

He grips my neck then, wrapping his fingers around my taut skin. "Please, Reece, fuck me harder," I groan, my voice raspy from his grip around my windpipe.

He groans, his other hand sliding to my waist as he requests, "Get on your knees, and face the window."

I give him a quizzical look, but follow his request quickly. I don't dare turn to face him, but can hear his breathing. This encounter is turning me on. My curtain is wide open and it's dusk, so anyone outside could see my hard dick through the window. Could see Reece siding up behind me, as I feel his dick slipping between my crease and teasing my pucker again.

"Hands on the window, pretty boy."

I press my sweaty hands against the window, and Reece slips inside my hole, grabbing my waist with his hands as he begins to rut inside me.

"Oh god, Reece, more, harder, fuck!" I roar, matching his thrusts back and forth. I turn my head and kiss him.

Kissing me back, Reece laves his tongue over my lips demanding entrance to invade my mouth, to deepen the intense kiss that has my heart racing and my whole body thrumming with the desire only Reece Montserrat, my once but no longer enemy can bring out in me.

I moan into his mouth and he shoves me forward with a deep thrust, stilling his hips a moment.

"You going to come for me, pretty boy?" Reece asks raspily after breaking the kiss.

"Yes, baby," I groan as he starts rocking in and out again, his hand dropping to my dick and stroking it in time with his thrusts.

"Who do you belong to, Capullo?" Reece questions, still with the raspiness to his voice.

"You, Reece," I groan, pushing back and causing a loud moan to escape his lips. It spurs me on, so I groan, "My body, my soul and my whole heart belong to you Reece Montserrat. I'm yours alone."

"Mine," Reece grunts, his dick throbbing inside me indicating he's close to release. "You're fucking mine, Capullo and I'm going to paint your fucking insides with my cum."

I groan again, his dick once again hitting that spot. He's barely touching my dick but feeling his release deep inside my body is enough to set me alight, enough for me to paint the window with my cum. Reece grabs my waist, pulling me back as I ride out my orgasm, shivering and shooting ropes of cum all over the glass.

He pulls out and reaches out to wipe up the come on the window with his palm. He holds it out to me, with a wicked smirk on his face.

"Clean up your mess, you dirty boy." I lick his palm, and he groans before licking it himself and then kissing me, so hard I gasp for a breath against his lips. Still kissing we fall back against the bed. I entangle my legs with his, and with a gasp for breath, I break the kiss.

"I love you, Reece."

"I love you, more, Jasper," he says sweetly, kissing my forehead. The gesture makes me feel cherished.

"Will you come with me tomorrow?"

"Of course, I'll come with you tomorrow," Reece chuckles. "We're going to come together every damn day for the rest of our lives, Capullo."

I burst out laughing, partly at Reece's response and partly at myself for not realising my question had a sexual connotation.

"No, idiot, I meant will you come with me to my parents' house to snoop?"

"Well yeah, of course, but also sex will be happening because I'm not fucking kidding pretty boy. I'm going to make you come every day for the rest of our lives."

He kisses me again to seal the promise against my lips.

"I can't wait," I reply against his lips, reaching down to pull the sheet up over our bodies. I don't want to share my true thoughts with Reece right now. The fear that this is going to be the last time we're together. Delving into our family's past—the feud—may tear us apart and I'm petrified of losing Reece, scared of the spiral that will send me into. I've kept my drug use to a minimum, but temptation has always been there and now I've experienced pleasure of a different kind I don't think I could face losing that without seeking pleasure in another way.

I cradle back into Reece's arms, let him hold me close whilst I drift to sleep. Hopefully, I'm worrying for nothing, and soon I'll be able to love Reece openly.

It's a risk to come to my parent's house, to sneak into my father's office with Reece by my side. Thankfully I know his routine like clockwork and he's currently at the country club, drinking with his associates until late evening.

Mum isn't as predictable with her movements, but entering the house it's silent and if mum was home without my father around, there'd most likely be soft jazz playing from the parlour.

Even so we tiptoe down the hallway, avoiding the creaky floorboards to enter my father's office.

Every surface, the bookshelves and the huge oak desk are immaculate. There is not one piece of paperwork in sight or anything out of place.

Reece scoffs under his breath. "Fuck me, this office is like a damn museum."

"I know. My father is pedantic and everything has a place."

"You don't say. How in the hell are we going to find anything incriminating?"

I snigger, taking Reece's hand to drag him over towards the desk.

"I happen to know that father doesn't believe in locking things away. We're sure to find something in his desk drawers or the filing cabinet."

Reece nods, sliding open the desk drawer whilst I investigate the filing cabinet. It's neatly organised with file folders, and at first nothing seems out of the ordinary.

I'm frustrated by that. I don't really know what I'm looking for on this snooping expedition, but I know there has to be something useful.

Reece slams the door closed, and steps up behind me. His arms wrap around me and he leans on my shoulder.

"Find anything pretty boy?" he asks.

I turn back to give him a kiss. "Not yet, but there has to be something here. There's so many files and folders of paperwork."

"True," Reece responds, as I flick through a wad of papers in an unmarked file. "Those look suspicious."

I pull them out, close the filing cabinet with my hip, and spread out the pages on the desk. My eyes boggle as I glance over the documents.

"Shit, these aren't just any random pieces of paperwork, Jasp," Reece remarks, picking up one and studying it.

"You don't say. What's that one?"

"It's a copy of the deed to the Cassidy club. Your father sold it to mine."

"That's crazy," I respond, shaking my head because I can't believe it. It seems our parents have been doing dodgy deals between each other amidst this so-called feud for years. Their being enemies is all about the money. I hold up the document I'm scanning. "Look, this is bank statements detailing payments into foreign accounts with the Cassidy club being a source."

Reece scoffs and shakes his head. "Our parents are fucking hypocrites. Preaching to us, and the whole of Vemore that they're enemies but it's false."

"Which is why we need to get them to own up to their lies," I say, turning my back to face the photocopier behind me. I take a copy of the bank statements and the deed before filing them again as though I haven't touched them.

"We should get something to wipe our fingerprints off the drawers and cabinets."

I nod, affirming his words. "There's some alcohol wipes in the first aid kit."

"That'll work," Reece affirms, giving me a quick kiss as I head out to the kitchen to grab the first kit from under the sink.

Taking a few alcohol wipes back into my father's office, I quickly wipe over the drawers and the filing cabinet so they look completely untouched.

I stuff them into my pockets, and take Reece's hand in mine to leave the office. He snacthes them out, laughing. "You need to wipe the door handle too, pretty boy."

I laugh under my breath. "Oh yeah."

"Clearly you've never committed a crime, Capullo. You'd get caught for sure."

"Probably," I respond with a low laugh. "Do you need to head straight back to the dorms? Or wanna hang out in my room for a bit?"

"What's on offer if we hang out?"

"I might have some weed we can share, if you're down."

"I'm down," Reece responds, squeezing my hand. "If I get to fuck you whilst we're high?"

I drag him to my room, pushing him down onto the bed and kissing him.

"You can fuck me anytime, baby," I tease, kissing him harder and revelling in the taste of his mouth. The thought of fucking him whilst we're high already has my dick stirring in my pants. I'm a fiend for Reece Montserrat's dick.

CHAPTER THIRTY-NINE

Jasper

In the Art room after hours, I'm trying to paint Reece for my end of semester piece. He's shirtless, wearing only grey sweats and is staring at me with a wicked smirk whilst I try to concentrate on the painting. It's near impossible because Reece is a distraction at any time, and even more so when he's half naked and giving me a smirk that makes my stomach flip with the lust I feel for him.

He's insatiable.

"Stop, Ree," I plead, slapping his arm and forcing him to look at me.

"Stop what, Jasp?" he taunts, winking at me and then licking his lips.

"You know what you're doing, Reece Montserrat."

"I'm not doing anything. You're the one doing the painting."

"You're taunting me, Reece."

"I'd never," he sasses, spreading his legs wide to show that he's hard beneath his sweats.

"Your dick is hard, Ree."

He slides a hand inside his sweats, groaning as he starts stroking himself, all the while staring at me.

"Mmm, so good," he moans, halting his strokes as he leans forward, closer to me. Gulping— anticipating his kiss—I squeeze the tip of the paintbrush in my grip tightly and spurt paint over Reece's bare chest.

He laughs and leans even closer to me, rasping against my lips, "Are you trying to get me dirty, Capullo?"

I kiss him back a moment and throw his words from earlier back at him, "I'd never."

Again he laughs, this time it's laced with a dirty undertone. "You just want me naked, pretty boy, admit it?"

I groan, leaning forward and kissing him, whilst simultaneously pushing him down onto his back. He grips the linen floor mat with one hand to steady himself, and grabs the strap of my overalls with his other hand.

He moans into the kiss, tearing his mouth from mine to rasp, "Get naked, pretty boy."

"What if someone comes in?" I question, biting down on my lip nervously.

"Then they'll got one hell of a free show," he responds without hesitation as he yanks off his sweats. I'm still processing his request and admiring his body, his hard dick.

"Jasper, get naked now, and get on all fours," Reece demands, shoving me slightly to spur me on. Staring at him, I slide the straps of my overalls down my shoulders, unclipping them and standing to shimmy them over my hips so they fall down my legs to the floor. I yank my paint covered white t-shirt over my head, and throw it at Reece. He clasps it, sniffing it a moment before throwing it across the room, and staring up at me in only my boxers.

"I said get naked and get on fours, Capullo."

With my gaze on his, I slide my boxers down my legs. I step out of them and kick them and my overalls aside. Reece grunts in annoyance that I'm not obeying his request to get on all fours.

"Jasper," he rasps, gripping my calves and attempting to pull me down.

I give him the control and let my legs give out, dropping to my knees in front of him. He grips my dick a moment, and kisses me, murmuring into my mouth, "All fours now."

I obey, turning around so my arse is in his face. He kisses my cheek, sucking the flesh so he leaves a mark on my skin.

He then picks up a paintbrush, brushing it across my cheeks. It's slightly scratchy but tickles as well. Dipping it in the red paint, Reece then paints on my butt. The paint is cold, and it causes me to shiver with every stroke. I can't work out what he's painted but it feels like words.

"What did you write, Ree?" I ask, nodding at him.

Reece laughs and gives me a smirk, before replying, "This sexy arse belongs to Reece."

He kneels behind me, lining up his dick with my pucker. He slaps my butt, leaning over to kiss away the sting. He slaps my butt cheek again, this time slathering paint over my pucker, and teasing me with his finger. It feels cold, and odd but I don't have a moment to think further about it before Reece is sliding inside my hole. He grips my hips, and thrusts in and out slowly, teasingly.

I arch my back, calling out, "Oh fuck, Reece! Feels so good."

He slaps my butt again, and pulls all the way out. The withdrawal of his dick causes a deep emptiness to overtake me.

I want to protest, and turn to look back at him.

"Don't pout, pretty boy."

"Why'd you stop fucking me?"

Reece gives me a sexy smirk in response, before he murmurs, "Because I want you to sit on my cock, and ride me until you're painting this art room with cum."

He reaches forward and pulls me into his lap.

I gasp at the contact of his hard dick against my taint.

"Spread your legs, and ride me, Jasper," Reece murmurs, opening his legs a little to cause me to spread mine. Rising up onto my tiptoes, I grip his dick at the base and press it against my pucker, slowly lowering myself onto his length. He moans lasciviously, and grips my hips, guiding me up and down as I fuck myself on his dick. I still my movement a moment, when my balls meet his.

"Who said you could stop, Jasp," Reece taunts, fucking upwards into me so hard I groan, murmuring out almost incoherently, "ffffuuccccckkkk!"

This position feels beyond incredible and with one hard thrust that hits my prostate I come, grabbing my dick at the last minute to control the spurts of come that are covering the floor. The last drops hit my stomach, and Reece groans, filling my hole with his release. The throbbing of his dick inside me causes another shiver—an aftershock—of pleasure to course through me, and I coat myself in even more come. I slide off Reece's dick, and collapse beside him, sighing deeply.

CAZ MAY

"You came twice?" he asks, glancing at my come covered stomach.

"Yeah, that was fucking incredible, Ree," I reply, feeling my cheeks heat with a blush. Reece bends down and laves his tongue over my skin, cleaning the come off with his tongue. He stretches up to kiss me after, and tasting myself on my tongue causes me to moan, and bite his lip to draw some blood. He licks that away, and breaks the kiss with a groan.

I cup his cheeks in my hands. "I love you, Reece."

"I love you, my pretty boy." He kisses me again, just a sweet, caring type of kiss that causes my heart to race.

"I think you should make peace with Tidus. Get him to see that our love is real."

He nods, giving me a peck of a kiss. "If you wish it so, Jasp. I'd do anything for you. I love you so fucking much, Jasper Capullo."

"I love you just as fucking much, maybe more, Reece Montserrat."

We kiss again then, just enjoying kissing for awhile before we clean up. He wipes the residual paint off my body with the floor cloth, and we tug our clothes back on before packing up the paint and brushes. I put them back in my basket, and hook it over my arm, whilst holding the canvas under my arm. It's a complete mess, and I'm going to have to start again–and paint it from memory–without Reece around to distract me. He takes my other hand and we head out into the cool night air. I hate that I can only hold his hand now in the darkness, but hopefully soon we can be completely open with our love for each other.

CHAPTER FORTY

REECE

I'd told Jasper that I'd make peace with Tidus–about him catching me fucking his cousin–in the aftermath of our hot fuck session in the art room. But now that I'm driving around the Capullo side of Vemore in search of Tidus, it seems like a foolish idea. And I'm definitely not feeling keen about it at all.

Jasper had informed me of his cousin's usual hangouts, and true to form I find the blonde idiot at the abandoned ruin of the old docks. He's smoking a joint, sitting down and staring into the ocean. I'm not surprised by that, but I'm taken aback by the person sitting next to him, who takes the joint from him and inhales it, blowing smoke across to Tidus with a smirk on his face.

Something is going on between them, and I'm pissed off with Malyk for not telling me he's been hanging out with Tidus. I've been open with my best friend about my feelings—my sex life—with Jasper and he's hiding his, or what appears to be his from me.

I should be calm for the conversation I need to have with Jasper's cousin, but getting out of my car I'm seething, curling my fists ready for a fight.

Stepping up towards them I inhale a deep breath, giving my best friend a death glare.

"What are you doing here with the enemy, Mal?" I taunt him, shoving him as he stands.

"Nothing, my sweet. Just keeping the peace."

Tidus stands, dropping the spent joint to the sand and butting it out with the steel cap of his boot.

"Lay off him, Montserrat."

I shove Malyk aside, turning my focus towards Tidus and taunting him, "Why Tidus? You got the hots for Mal, huh?"

"Fuck no! I'm not a homo like you." His words are full of malice. Malyk's face falls, as though Tidus has punched him right in the feels.

"Right, and like Jasper?"

"My cousin will drop you, homo. He's not like you."

I laugh. "Oh, but he is, Tidus. Jasper loves me, and you need to get used to it."

"The fuck I will!" Tidus seethes, shoving me, and drawing his gun, cocking it at me, pointing directly at my heart.

"You going to shoot the man your dear cousin is in love with?"

"You don't deserve him. You're a Montserrat, scum of Vemore."

"You speak of yourself if you take away the love of his life. He will hate you."

The reality of my words hits him. And he drops his gun, instead he launches himself towards me, knocking me to the ground.

"Take it back," he taunts in my face, his breathing ragged.

"Relent Tidus, I'm only trying to make peace with you. I love Jasper, and I don't want to fight with you or your family any longer."

"But you've made him change. That is not love."

"I've not done anything you speak of. I've simply fallen in love with my enemy."

"You're the fucking enemy!" he growls, punching my jaw.

"The fuck, Tidus!" I screech, shoving him off me. He stumbles, tripping over his gun. Leaning down he picks it up, again cocking it at me. I glance at my best friend, giving him a pleading help me look.

"Mal, have you nothing to say?"

He shakes his head, then steps up to my side.

"I'm not going to side with either of you. You're both fighting for the same, both admitting wrong, and I will not be a part of this feud."

I'm flabbergasted, and admittedly Tidus is too. He scoffs and stares daggers at Malyk before coming at me again. "You will leave my cousin alone, or so help me I will end this feud with taking your life."

"Do it, Tidus," I taunt, daring him to pull the trigger of the gun. He's barely a metre away from both Malyk and me. If he shoots, we're likely to both get hurt and die out here on the beach in Capullo territory. I take a step back, still daring Tidus with my glare.

I watch Tidus, my gaze dropping between his intense stare and the finger that pulls back on the trigger. My heart races. This will be the end of me, the last breath I take. Thoughts of Jasper fill my mind and I close my eyes, exhaling the breath as the shot rings out in the air.

"Fuck! You shot me, you dick!" Malyk's raspy voice screeches from beside me, where he's dropped to the ground, clutching his stomach. Tidus screams, so loudly the sound bounces off the stone of the ruins surrounding us.

"No! I…fuck!" he bellows, dropping to Malyk's side on his knees, pressing his hands against his stomach to curb the bleeding. Malyk is gasping for breath. And Tidus is distraught. "Malyk, fuck, Malyk, I'm sorry. I…I fuck…I…" he stammers, leaning down over Malyk as tears stream down his face.

I'm fuming. The feud is not over, and my best friend is fighting for life for something that should not involve him. I drag Tidus to his feet and slap him across the cheek.

"If he fucking dies, I'll fucking torture you until you're begging for me to end your life."

"I'm sorry Reece. I don't know what else to say."

The sirens start then, screaming their way towards us. The ambulance pulls up at the far end of the beach, only a metre from my car. I lean into Tidus' side. "We need to leave now, or his death may very well be on your hands."

Tidus gives me a nod, but his eyes as he picks up his gun from the ground beside Malyk give me an uneasy feeling. He's a two-faced prick, and I get the feeling his grievance with me is not over.

Getting in my car, the moment the Bluetooth connects I speed dial Barth.

"Cuz, what up?" he answers after the third ring, whilst I'm racing off towards Montserrat territory.

"Mal...he...he...got shot," I stammer, trying to hold back my tears.

"You're fucking shitting me? Who?" Bartholomew asks, his tone full of malice.

"Tidus fucking Capullo."

"Oh, shit," Barth gasps. "Why'd he shoot ya boy?"

"Because he caught Jasper and me together, and like the good boyfriend I am, at Jasper's request I went to make peace with his cousin."

"And how does that involve Malyk?"

I sigh, careening around a corner, sure that someone is following me. "It's complicated," I voice, laying off the accelerator a little to slow the car down. "You at the club?"

"Nah, mine cuz."

"I'm coming to get you. Be there in ten."

"Sweet, cuz. Catch ya soon," he says, hanging up.

Gunning it again, I take the last corner to head to Bartholomew's house. His digs are pretty sweet, his very own flat behind his parents' house that faces the beach.

When I arrive, he's waiting out the front of the iron gates. I come to a stop and press the door open button. His door rises open and he slides in, clicking his seatbelt into place as the door closes.

"Hey cuz, you ok?"

"Yeah, just a bit shaken. I'm scared Mal is going to die." I realise with my words that my breathing is laboured, on the verge of a panic attack.

Barth places a hand on my thigh. "He'll be fine, cuz. Mal is a strong fucker. I can't see a bullet wound taking him down."

"I fucking hope so, Barth. I can't lose him, even though he drives me crazy sometimes. He's like my brother."

"I know, he'll be fine," Barth reassures me, glancing backwards to look out the rear windscreen.

I tilt my eyes towards the rear vision mirror, and nod to Barth. "We're being followed, cuz."

"It's fucking Tidus. Have you got your gun on you?"

He taps his hip. "Of course, cuz."

I press the electric window engage button, and it slides down. Barth unclips his seatbelt, withdrawing his gun from his belt. He leans out the window, and shoots towards Tidus' car behind us. His car skids, before he speeds up and aligns his car with mine. His window rolls down, and he fires a shot towards Barth. It misses, hitting the side of my car instead. Barth shrinks back into the seat.

"Drive cuz, your car is faster than his piece of shit Merc."

I thrash the engine, sending the speedometer towards two hundred. Barth fires another shot out the window, and the sound of it hitting metal reverberates around the street.

The next few minutes are a complete blur. I haven't turned on my headlamps and it's nearing dark. Shots are being fired, left and right, by Barth and Tidus, or his fucking minions. But it's the hiss that is the most prominent sound, causing me to lose control of the car when Tidus fires a shot into my front tyre. The screech of my patent black rims colliding with the bitumen is ear splitting, and I scream out, "Fuck!" as I mount the curb and collide with the traffic lights. Barth and I jump out of the car. I'm irate. The fucker has not only killed–or hopefully ingured–my best friend but he's also caused me to total my car. And for what? Falling in love with his cousin, as though that is a crime.

Tidus comes screeching to a stop, crashing into the back of my car to thoroughly crush it, slamming it further into the pole. I can't even be satisfied with him totalling his car, because mine is beyond repair now. He gets out of his car, and spits on the ground, whilst butting out the cigarette he throws on the ground at his feet.

I draw my gun, and stalk towards him.

"You fucking piece of shit! You totalled my Bugatti!"

"Worth it," Tidus snarls. "You'll have no means to get to Jasper. I'll kill you myself and tell my cousin you died in the firey wreck of your car," he growls, just as my car erupts into flames. I want to cry–fucking cry–like a damn fool. I should be happy right now, I should be with Jasper enjoying being in love, but instead I'm here watching the car I love–and can't replace–turning into a fireball.

"You're heartless, Tidus. You'll break your cousin's heart with your malice."

He points the gun at me, and even in the darkness I can see his pupils are dilated with rage. There is silence surrounding us, only the hiss of the fire so I hear Tidus pull back on the trigger of his gun. I do the same, and close my eyes as I fire the gun.

"Fuck, cuz, fuck." My heart stops a moemnt, and I open my eyes to find Barth in front of me, clutching his side, his other hand limply by his with his gun only barely in his grip. I accidentally shot Bartholomew.

"Shit, Barth, I...."

"You didn't, cuz. It was Tidus." I'm speechless, glancing around to find Tidus also on the ground, having been shot as well. Who shot who isn't clear, but Tidus is bleeding, lying lifeless on the ground. I should help him, but instead I snake an arm around my cousin's waist, and help him over to the curb.

It's like déjà vu–from a mere hour ago–with sirens coming towards us.

"Go cuz, I'll be ok. Make sure Malyk is ok."

Nodding I run away from the scene, scared that I've killed Tidus. It's a fucking long way back into Capullo territory from this side of the city, but I keep running. I need to see Jasper. We need to end this feud for good. And even though I'm scared shitless about the consequences of tonight's events, we need to confront them head on–together–by admitting everything to our parents. I'd burn the world down, and kill anyone–even family–to be with Jasper.

CHAPTER FORTY-ONE

Jasper

My dorm room window screeches open, startling the bejesus out of me as my back is turned whilst I'm getting ready for bed.

Reece tumbles onto my bed, and he looks an absolute fright, as though he's witnessed death tonight. A surge of panic rushes through me, that increases tenfold when Reece sits on the edge of my bed—without even looking at me—and bursts into tears.

"Baby? What happened?" I question, sitting down on the bed and wrapping my arms around him, pulling him to my side. He cries against my shoulder, soaking the sleeve of my white t-shirt. Seeing him—my strong, rough man—like this is breaking my heart. Something has to be seriously wrong for Reece to be at breaking point.

"Ree, please tell me what's wrong?" I plead, kissing his forehead as I pull away slightly and he looks at me, biting down on his lip. "I can't bear seeing you like this."

"Mal…he…got…he…" he stammers, his voice raspy and panicked.

"He what baby? Is he ok?"

"I don't know," he cries out, completely shattering my heart.

"What happened, Reece?" I practically plead with him.

"He got shot. I went to speak to Tidus about us, and Mal was there. It turned into a fight." He's calmer now, but his voice is low, just a whisper.

"And you left Malyk there?"

"I had to. The cops and ambulance were coming. I couldn't have any blood on my hands."

"Makes sense. Where's Tidus now?"

"Fucked if I know. I got out of there. Alaric will have my head if he finds out I was involved."

Leaning forward I wrap an arm around his side and pull him close. He nuzzles into my side. Weirdly, I'm the one comforting him, but I'm not hating it. Seeing Reece showing a more vulnerable side is causing me to fall even harder for him.

"I love you, Jasp," he whispers, glancing at me with a meek smile.

"I love you more, Ree."

"I love it when you call me Ree, and love it more when you call me baby."

I chuckle softly, murmuring, "Baby." Reece groans, and I silence him with a kiss.

A few moments later he breaks the kiss, sighing deeply. "Do you think it's time?" he asks, puzzling me.

"Time for what?"

"Telling our families about us, together as a united front."

"If that's what you want then I'm open to it."

"I've told my dad already but we need to get them in the same room somehow."

I contemplate what he's saying for a moment. It certainly won't be easy to get our feuding parents to be somewhere at the same time, but I know of one place—mutual territory—that we may be able to get them to attend in the guise of a business opportunity neither of them could pass up.

"What're you thinking, Capullo?" Reece asks, snark in his tone.

"That we tell both our parents we've heard of a business opportunity to buy Perlu Beach Club, and their presence is required there to meet with the vendor and present an offer."

Reece scowls. "That's a long shot, Jasp."

"Yeah, but it just might work. It's mutual territory and both of our families want to steal it out from under the Murphys'."

"Let's do it," Reece responds, sounding way more positive than I'm feeling. This has to work because I don't want to be without Reece in my life. Just the thought of that hurts way too much.

The conference room of Perlu Beach Club is huge. There's a large table taking up the entire centre of the room, with black swivelling leather chairs that are truly opulent. Occasional tables line the windows, and sheer lace curtains graze the floor covering the floor to ceiling windows that look out to the ocean.

Reece is holding my hand in his and squeezes it. "Didn't know the Murphy's had this much cash to splash around these days."

"Yeah, me neither," I reply, glancing at my boyfriend and then at the wooden ornate doors that are creaking open slightly as though someone is walking past them at speed. "Must be old money."

Reece nods in agreeance, drawing in a breath as the doors careen open and first my father–with my mother trailing behind–barrels into the room. He's already seething, and I gulp back the lump that's formed in my throat. This is not a good start.

Only a few seconds later, Reece's parents are in the room, and it's death glares all around, both of our father's gazes locked on each other in a battle of dominance without the exchange of words. My heart is racing, and my hand in Reece's is clammy. It was stupid to think putting them in the same room was a good idea. I'm afraid they're about to draw arms and shoot each other down for daring to set foot in the same space as each other. Although that would result in death, I'm not entirely convinced that's a bad thing. Reece and I could love each other in relative peace, but it would be at the cost of death, and that's not what I want.

My father's gaze finds me, his scowl deepening. "Jasper!" he roars, "What is the meaning of this? Why have you dragged your mother and I here?"

I drop Reece's hand and take a step towards my father. My heart is still in overdrive, but I need to do this. "I brought you and mother here today to confess to you both that I'm in love with Reece Montserrat and no longer wish to marry anyone of your choosing."

"What absolute trollop, Jasper Terence. You cannot love a man, and most certainly cannot love your sworn enemy."

I scoff, retaking Reece's hand as he steps up next to me. We're a united front against our parents. "Reece is not my enemy, father. Being enemies with the Montserrat's isn't on us, it's on you."

He starts to speak, but Reece's father bellows, "You're speaking heresy, boy. I've ordered kills for less."

"Cut the bullshit, father," Reece responds, his voice harsh.

"Bite your tongue, son. And drop the hand of your enemy."

"And what if I don't?" Reece taunts his father, his eyebrows quirking up.

"Then I may cut it off, and feed it to the wolves of Stockade Road."

Reece shrinks back, his bravado shot down by the literal words his father just spoke. Stockade Road is as far from the world of Vemore as we know. It's where the cityscape meets the forest and is said to be haunted by our ancestors who dared to go beyond the city limits. They met their fate at the mouths of wolves.

The room is now enveloped in silence and it's my father who speaks first, "Do you declare that you love my son, Reece Montserrat?"

The word 'love' and Reece's name on my father's tongue come out as though he's spitting out poison.

Reece stares my father dead in the eye, responding, "Yes, Mr Capullo. I love Jasper with every piece of my soul."

Mr Montserrat scoffs, and Reece glares at him. "You don't have a soul, son. Like father, like son."

My father fixes his gaze back on me. "See, Jasper. There is no love here, and you will not seek it out. You're to stay apart and not bring any blasphemy to our name."

I stalk towards my father, my blood suddenly boiling with what he's asking of me.

"Fuck you, father!" I roar, shoving him hard, pushing my open palms into his chest. He barely moves, so I shove him again, practically screaming, "I'll kill myself if I'm kept from Reece."

My father barely flinches at my words, instead, he takes my hand and drags me out of the room. I only get to look back at Reece through the corner of my eye. He's crying and my heart is shattered. I don't want to be alive anymore. Being alive without Reece by my side is no life worth living.

I'd had to beg, and scream the house down for my parents to allow me to go back to the dorms. They'd barely let me out of their sight and had confiscated my phone so I wasn't able to contact Reece, and had no way of knowing about what was happening in the outside world. I was missing my classes, hating that I was going to possibly fail my art project–because I'd left all the supplies I'd needed in my dorm room–but mostly I was missing

Reece. I felt empty without him. A shell of my former self. At first, I thought I was a sinner for being with him, but the way I feel for Reece–the love I have for him–makes me feel complete and whole, and expressing love is no sin. Reece is also my vice. I need him.

I can't have him now though, and I can't even leave the dorm room as my father has guards watching my every move–who know my schedule–and also know exactly what Reece looks like. He couldn't sneak in here right now even if he wanted to.

It's probably not a good idea to be seeking out Blaise right now when I'm in a vulnerable state, but being without Reece is painful. I just want to feel something–anything–for the pain to be gone for even a moment. Blaise is known around Vemore–especially in the university dorms–for selling all manner of illicit drugs, as well as prescription painkillers and antidepressants. Where he gets them I've honestly got no idea, but right now I don't care where he gets them, only that he can.

I don't have a phone, but Blaise is always in the dining hall for supper and that is one place I can actually go other than classes. I'll still be watched, however, they'll just think I'm talking to a friend.

I shove a wad of cash into my jeans pocket, as I tug them on and yank on a t-shirt as I rush out of my dorm room. My father's lackeys eye me suspiciously, following me quickly like lost dogs.

After grabbing my supper of Spaghetti bolognese I spot Blaise across the room and rush over to sit next to him before someone else snags the seat. He always sits under the window that looks out onto the courtyard, and it's a popular seat if you can get it.

He nods at me, scooping a heaped forkful of spaghetti into his mouth.

"Hey Blaise," I greet him, screwing the lid of my bottle of water and taking a sip.

He gulps down his mouthful of spaghetti, and replies, "Hi Jasp. You doing ok?"

I shake my head. "No, I'm not."

I twirl my fork through my spaghetti, biting down on it and slurping it. It tastes good, but food isn't going to take away the ache in my stomach and heart.

"That's no good. Want something to take the edge off?" he asks, quirking his eyebrow up at me with his suggestive tone.

"You got any painkillers or Xanax?"

"Always, bro. Got both."

"I'll have both. Bring them to my room after supper," I request, yanking the cash out and waving it at him.

He nods again, grabbing it under the table and slipping it into his pocket. We both finish eating our spaghetti in relative silence, except for the slurping of the spaghetti.

Since coming back from the dining hall, I'm pacing my room waiting for Blaise to arrive with the drugs. I know I shouldn't be contemplating taking anything not prescribed to me, but I want the pain to go away. Being kept away from Reece has me so on edge I feel like scratching my skin raw to feel something. I can't cope with feeling so empty. If I can't take the pain away I want more pain–different pain–not heartbreak. Heartbreak is the worse kind of pain. It hurts more than when I broke my arm as a kid falling off my pushbike.

Glancing at the clock I notice I've only been back for about fifteen minutes, however it feels like it's been hours. Time is fickle lately. It's only been a week since everything happened and I was forced to not see Reece, although it feels like it's been months, years even. Even a day without him would be–is–torture I've had my fill of feeling. I grab a bottle of vodka from my closet. It's only half full and I have no idea when I opened it. It doesn't matter. It will go down like water anyway.

I'm just screwing the lid off when there's a rap of knuckles on my dorm room door. I open it to find

Blaise smiling until he sees me. I'd stripped off so all I'm wearing is grey sweats with paint stains down the legs.

"Eww, dude. You could wear something."

I scoff under my breath. "I'm wearing sweats. Have you got the stuff?" I ask, glancing around him, up and down the hallway to make sure no one is watching.

"Yep, got you some extra…" he starts speaking rather loudly, and I grab his arm to tug him into my room. I push it closed hard, and glare at him.

"Seriously , Blaise. Have you no tact. Someone could hear you."

"Sorry. But you need to relax dude."

Again I scoff at him. "Hence why I need the damn tablets, idiot."

He scowls at me, clearly offended by my name calling but I couldn't care less. I just need the drugs now.

He shoves his hand into his pocket, pulling out three tiny ziplock bags with five or so pills in each. He waves them in front of my face, a wicked smirk on his face that has me worried for a moment. The worry is short lived though, and I snatch the bags from his grip.

"Thanks, Blaise."

"Anytime, Jasper. Enjoy your high."

I plonk down on the end of the bed, and he sees himself out. I don't even look up at the door—hoping in passing that he actually closed it—as I open the ziplock bags and tip the contents out onto the duvet.

I have no idea which ones are which, and frankly I don't care. I screw off the cap from the vodka, and scoop up a handful of the tablets, tipping them into my open mouth before taking a swig of vodka to swallow them down. It burns. Kinda in a good, numbing type of way though.

I repeat the process with the remaining tablets, gulping down the rest of the vodka until my throat feels numb and my head starts spinning. I lay back on the pillow, and close my eyes, spreading myself out on the bed to drift away and forget about the pain of not being with Reece.

CHAPTER FORTY-TWO

REECE

The past week —without Jasper by my side—has been absolutely crucifying. I'm empty without him and my head is filled with words of anguish. The dickhead who said love was beautiful was a liar. The only thing that made this week bearable was Malyk and Barthomelew being discharged from the hospital. They'd both suffered bullet wounds, but their surgery removed the bullets and thankfully hadn't done any damage to internal organs. Malyk had lost his spleen but a small price to pay for him being alive. No one even knows what the fuck a spleen is for anyway. I'm sure he won't miss it.

Other than seeing them both when they got discharged, I've kept to myself to wallow in self-pity of being unable to see Jasper. I'd tried to sneak into Valley View a few times, but there were now armed fucking guards everywhere, stalking around the campus like they were protecting royalty.

I'm definitely on edge, and worried about Jasper. Not being able to see him just makes me uneasy. And I can't get out of my head. I'm also ignoring my father, not willing to do his damn bidding anymore. I'm not that man anymore. I don't care if I never see him again. I won't be so lucky, but it's nice to think about.

To escape I'm at the furthest beach from the Capullo side of the city, as I can be. Velum Beach is pristine white sand and has some of the biggest waves of any beach in Vemore.

Sitting on the sand with my open journal in my lap, I'm staring at the blank page in front of me. I've hardly used it since being with Jasper, because my pretty boy has been my vice and my escape when I've needed to get out of my head. But now I feel like casting it aside and running into the ocean to drown myself. Living without Jasper causes a deep emptiness within me. I don't move though, instead I scrawl words across the page.

Emptiness. Crushed. Loveless. Shattered.

The words I've written break my heart more. I love Jasper, but we're being forced to be absent from each other's lives because our parents can't accept our love and get over a feud that doesn't involve us, or them quite frankly. There's no reason for our families to still be feuding, years later.

Slamming my journal closed, I wipe an arm across my cheeks to wipe away the tears on my cheeks. I can't believe I'm crying, but I've truly never felt such heartbreak. We didn't break up–per se–but it feels as though we have.

Standing from the sand, I'm shocked to find Blaise running towards me frantically.

"Reece! I...fucked up!" he calls out, stopping in front of me, and scuffing his feet in the sand.

"How? What did you do dickhead?"

"I think something has happened to Jasper."

"How in the hell would you know that? And what the fuck do you mean, Blaise?"

"Well, you know I'm going to Valley Views as I am not of feuding family blood, and well..."

I grab the front of his shirt and tug him closer. "What does your attendance there have to do with Jasper?"

"I know about you guys." I can feel the blood fall from my face. I'm not ashamed of my being with Jasper, but if Blaise knows then we haven't hidden our love from anyone.

"Ok, still doesn't explain the current situation of you seeking me out."

"Well, I um...gave him something to take the edge off."

"You gave him drugs?"

"Yeah, he sought me out and asked for Xanax and strong painkillers."

"And you gave him them?"

"Sold them to him. How is this news to you?"

"I had my suspicions about you dealing, but had no confirmation so you've not been unlucky enough to grace my hit list."

He gulps audibly, mumbling, "I might be now."

"What did you do, Blaise? Tell me now or I'll shoot you right here on the beach for bats to devour."

"I just got word from my source that the pills were laced."

I shove him away, my heart pounding with apprehension.

"With what?"

Blaise drops his gaze to the sand, again mumbling, "with rat poison."

I scream, shoving Blaise to the ground and stomping towards my car. He stumbles over, yanking the door open with strength I didn't know he had. I'd give anything to have my Bugatti right now. He wouldn't have been able to get into that without my letting him, but all I've got is a shitty ninety eigthies Audi a5 that my father had stashed in the garage as though it was prize relic of a car. It's older than me, and sputters as though it has smokers lungs when you start it. I don't say a word to Blaise as I drive off with him gripping the dashboard for dear life.

I speed into Vemore, stopping just outside of town.

"Get out of the car, Blaise."

He stares at me blankly. "I'm sorry, Reece. I didn't know."

"I don't give a fucking shit Blaise. If Jasper dies, it's on you."

His cheeks pale, and again I request, "Get out of my car." He nods, obeying this time and opening the door. He leans in the open door. "I'm sorry. Let me know if he's ok."

"Not likely," I snap, adding snidely, "And don't follow me."

He slams my door shut, stepping around the bonnet of my car to walk away. I shouldn't even consider what I'm about to do, but I'm pressing my foot down on the accelerator before I can think otherwise, causing Blaise to tumble to the ground with a bellowing scream and shrieking words that I can't understand. My breathing has kicked up a notch, coming out in panting, raspy, ragged breaths. Again I press down on the accelerator, this time driving straight over Blaise's body on the ground. I hear the crunch and crack of his breaking bones as I'm running him over, but I don't give a fuck.

All that matters now is getting to Jasper. My heart is constricting. If Jasper is dead I can only hope there's still some pills left for me.

Arriving at Valley View university I drive straight into the courtyard, through the gates at speed, not giving a fuck that the guards that are protecting my man are forced to scramble away. Cutting the engine, I get out of the car, and run towards the dorms, leaping over the tables and seats in my path. I can sense the guards on my tail, but I ignore them. Crashing through the double doors into the dorms I race down the hallway, shoving anyone in my path aside without a care. There's chaos all around me, yelling voices that are most definitely my name but all I care about it getting to Jasper's room. Reaching it, I knock loudly until my knuckles hurt whilst screaming his name at the top of my lungs. But there's no response.

Taking a step back I extend my leg, and kick the door right at the lock to bust it. Thankfully it's weak and gives way easily, allowing me to push the door open to enter the room.

I don't even close the door behind me, my mouth falling open as I take in the sight in front of me. Jasper is sprawled out across his bed, his arm and leg hanging over the edge and he's only in paint covered grey sweatpants. There's an empty vodka bottle on the floor beside the bed–as though he's just dropped it from his grip–and there's ziplock bags between his spread legs on the duvet. I kneel on the floor by the bed, touching the back of my hand to his forehead. His skin is clammy and cold. Gripping his hips, I shake him to force him to rouse. "Jasp, baby, wake up."

He doesn't even move, and makes no sound. I'm beginning to panic. Leaning over I put my head down over his heart, and take a sigh of relief that it's still beating, although slowly. He's unconscious but still alive, breathing shallowly but still taking in some breaths.

Again I give him a shake, lifting him up into a sitting position which is too easy. He's floppy, and practically weightless in my arms. "Jasper, please, wake up," I plead, but still he's unresponsive. I put him back on the bed, and turn to the door that has someone unfamiliar stumbling in.

He stalks towards me. "You need to get out!"

I stand, and face the stranger. "No! You need to call a damn ambulance. And I'm not leaving his side. If he dies I'll be right there beside the man I love when he takes his last breath."

He looks towards Jasper lying lifeless on the bed. "An ambulance?"

"Yes, he's unconscious idiot, and taken drugs that may have been laced with rat poison."

"Oh gosh," the man says, rushing into the room and staring down at him.

Again I seethe, "Call the fucking ambulance idiot."

He pulls a phone out of his pocket and dials emergency. I hear his responses to the questions, sitting back down next to Jasper and taking his hand in my mine. I lean over and kiss his forehead, whispering, "I love you, Jasper Capullo. You're going to ok, baby. It's you and me for evermore."

I stay there, laying down next to him and cradling him in my arms until it's a rush of activity with the ambulance officers rushing in and pulling him onto a stretcher. I follow them out, and climb into the back of the ambulance. No one dares question my presence on the way to the hospital. I intend to stay by his side until he wakes up, or until he takes his last breath. His last breath would be my last breath. Jasper Capullo is my whole world, my whole heart is his and if he survives this he'll be mine completely, in spite of our families. Jasper is the only one who matters.

CHAPTER FORTY-THREE

Jasper

My eyes feel heavy. I can't open them, and it's maddening. I can hear the beep of a heart monitor and hushed voices, some familiar and others not.

I want to scream out but the words—any sound— are caught in my throat, thanks to the oxygen mask I can feel on my face. I need it off. Now.

I lift my hand slightly but I don't have the strength to lift it to my face to pull the mask off.

"C'mon, Jasp, baby, wake up for me," Reece's voice pleads before he leans closer to whisper in my ear, "I miss fucking you."

His breath fanning over my ear as he exhales with those words causes a shiver to rush through me, goosebumps tingling my skin, my dick jolting. I need to wake up right now. I feel Reece shift again and he takes my hand, squeezing it. Behind the mask I gasp, forcing myself to inhale a deep before coercing myself to open my eyes.

They feel gritty and my vision is cloudy, but I can still see enough to dart my eyes around the room. I'm shocked to see my parents, as well as Reece's in the same room. They're all standing around the bed, whilst Reece is sitting in a chair by the side of the bed.

Coughing I gasp for air and Reece pulls the oxygen mask down to my chin. Leaning over he peppers my face with kisses, ending up leaving a faintly longer kiss on my lips that causes me to gasp.

He's openly kissing me with our parents in the room. Openly kissing me as though our parents are accepting of our love. I try to speak, but my throat is hoarse and it hurts like I've swallowed a hundred razor blades.

"It's ok, baby. You don't need to speak right now," Reece utters, kissing me again. I give in this time, kissing him back because I have my Reece back even just for a moment.

My parents could pull him out of the room and I'd be ok with that—at least for a little while—as I got to have another moment with him. Inhaling a deep breath I swallow hard.

"Reece, I can't believe you're here," I say hoarsely, my voice cracking from the strain of using it again and the emotions threatening to pull me under again.

CAZ MAY

"I've been here the whole time since you got admitted three days ago," he tells me, sniffing back tears. "I thought I was going to lose you, Jasper."

I gape at him. "Three days? Lose me?" I question, extremely puzzled as my head is a complete blur.

"Yeah, you overdosed on rat poison-laced pills and almost died. Don't you remember?"

"No, I...don't..." I stammer, shaking my head.

"It's ok, Jasp. You're okay now," he reassures me, squeezing my hand again and pressing a soft kiss to my forehead, causing a deep sigh to escape me.

"What? Pills?" I question shaking my head, trying to connect the dots.

"You bought pills from Blaise."

"Oh, shit. I...did," I remark, a memory crashing into my head from supper a few days ago when I confronted Blaise because I was missing Reece. I only have myself to blame. I'd never even thought about touching other drugs except weed before and never will after this. But I was at breaking point and that seemed like the only way out.

I look to Reece again. "It's ok Jasper. You're not in trouble."

"Really? I'm not going to get a fine for buying?"

"No, it's all handled," Reece replies with a wicked smirk.

I smile back. "What'd you do, baby?"

He leans in close and whispers gruffly, "I killed him for you, baby."

That sends a jolt of lust through me, and I kiss him again, murmuring against his lips, "I love you, Reece. Thank you."

He breaks the kiss, and whispers with his forehead to mine, "I'd kill anyone for you, baby."

He sits up, and glances around at our parents. He gives my father a nod, which causes him to round the bed and take my hand.

He exhales a deep breath. "We're sorry Jasper. Our feud should never have concerned you. And we've been selfish in not listening to you about your choice of love.

"Reece has been here by your bedside the whole time, and it was because of him that you're still with us. We cannot go on like this, feuding when it does our families no justice."

I sigh, not fully prepared to be accepting of my father's words.

"What are you saying, father?"

"We're drawing a line in it. The feud between the Capullo's and Montserrat's ends today."

I smile, glancing at Reece who nods, and pulls me close for a kiss as I sit up in the bed.

He then stands, and tips his head up to my father. "And your blessing still stands, right, Mr Capullo?"

My father extends a hand to Reece which he shakes firmly. "Yes Reece, you have my blessing to be with Jasper. You've shown me the unconditional love you have for my son, and I have witnessed the happiness you give each other."

I can't help but let out a squeal, nearly leaping off the bed to launch myself at my father to hug him.

"Thank you, father."

Breaking the hug, he smiles at me genuinely. "You do not need to thank me, son. I need to apologise for not seeing the real you."

"Never too late to see the light, father."

"Yes," he acknowledges, kissing my forehead. "We should be going now. Reece will arrange your discharge and we'll see you at home."

I nod, before accepting kisses from my mother, and Reece's parents before they leave the room.

"Thank fuck they're gone," I say with a laugh as Reece sits on the end of my bed.

"Yeah, you doing ok?"

"That was a lot right? I'm awake yeah?"

"Yeah, baby. You're not dreaming. It's really over."

"That's amazing, Ree. Thank you for smoothing things over with my family. I love you more than words could ever say."

He kisses me, and reaches down under the sheets, causing his hand to brush over the front of the itchy hospital gown.

He chuckles, taunting me, "Your dick is hard, pretty boy."

My cheeks colour, and I grab his wrist to stop him from stroking my length through the fabric. "Stop, Ree."

He gives me his wicked smirk. "You don't want me to make you come all over this hospital gown?"

I shake my head. "No, I want you to take me home, and fuck me all night."

He kisses me. "Then let's get you out of here, baby, so I can make you come until you beg me to stop."

Eagerly I press the call button behind me, and it's a flurry of activity with doctors and nurses coming in and fussing over me. I respond to the questions, awaiting the news that I can leave which comes quicker than expected.

Reece helps me dress into a hoodie–that smells like him–and some grey sweats. I shove my feet into sneakers and he takes my hand to lead me out. At the nurses station I sign some discharge papers, and Reece again takes my hand as we exit the hospital. The sunlight is bright but the warm rays feel amazing. I take a moment to revel in it, tugging up the sleeves of the hoodie.

"Ready to go home, baby?"

"More than ever. And hopefully soon my home will be with you."

"You never know what's around the corner, pretty boy."

He leads me to an unfamiliar car, and getting in I ask, "What happened to your Bugatti? Weren't you getting the gunshots fixed?"

He huffs as he slides in the drivers seat, buckling his seatbelt whilst I do the same.

"Your cousin caused me to total it into a fireball mess."

"Oh, Ree, I'm so sorry. But at least you're alive," I respond, taking his hand and squeezing it as he shifts through to first gear to drive away from the hospital. I can tell he doesn't want to discuss it more right now, and I'm not in the right headspace to hear it. I'm sure my parents would've told me if Tidus had died. The pain of that would've been written all over my mother's face.

We drive in silence the entire way back to my parents house, and the moment we're inside I drag Reece to my room. I've missed him so much, and I'm planning on spending the rest of the night showing him just how much.

CHAPTER FORTY-FOUR

REECE

Nerves are plaguing me as I drive to Velum Beach. Jasper is sitting beside me, clutching my hand in his and running his fingers over my palm. It's comforting but also causing my heart to race. He's also grinning at me, as though he knows something is up. I'd thought about asking him the night he was discharged from hospital and I stayed at his house but I wasn't organised. Now I had the necklace burning a hole in my pocket. I didn't want to go traditional and give him an engagement ring. It seems so cliched to me.

It seems like hours have passed when we pull up to the Velum beach carpark. As usual it's deserted, bar one car that looks like it's been parked for months and isn't going anywhere anytime soon.

I cut the engine and Jasper practically bolts out of the car. He runs onto the beach, stripping off his t-shirt and shorts as he runs towards the surf. I follow—not quite as eagerly—but I quickly catch up to him and wrap my arms around his waist from behind. He wriggles in my embrace.

"Jasp, baby, what are you doing?" I rasp into his ear.

He turns his head back to kiss me. "Going skinny dipping, Ree," he declares, a devilish smirk in his eyes that's taunting me, daring me to join him as he frees himself from my hold, and tugs his jocks down. He runs into the surf then, and I strip out of my clothes, watching—admiring—his bare arse. Once in the waves he splashes the water, beckoning me to join him. Cupping my dick I run into the waves, and pull him against me.

"Hey," he murmurs softly, giving me a shy kiss.

"Hey," I respond back, my voice raspier than I intended, showing that I'm turned on, despite the freezing water.

I kiss him harder, teasing him with my tip of my tongue. He moans into my mouth, and I deepen the kiss, exploring his mouth with strokes of my tongue against his. He groans and breaks the kiss. "Fuck, Reece. I love you."

"I love you too, Jasper. I'm so glad you're here with me, and I can be open with how much I adore you."

Our bodies are wrapped around each other, and we're bobbing up and down in the waves. He sighs. "I'm sorry for the choices I made. I didn't want to die. But I couldn't handle being apart from you. It was torture."

I kiss his forehead, replying, "You don't have anything to be sorry for, baby. It was torture, but it's the past and we need to look to the future."

His eyes light up with the word 'future' as though he knows exactly what I'm implying without saying it. Again I kiss him, hard and just as teasing as before. I bite down his lip, drawing a drop of blood that I lick away eagerly.

"Fuck," he hisses, breaking the kiss.

"You're mine, Jasper."

"Yours, Reece," he rasps back, shivering in my embrace.

"You cold?" I ask, squeezing his butt.

"Yeah, this water is freezing."

"Yeah, let's get out. I've got a surprise for you."

Again his eyes light up, and once I let him go he saunters out of the water, and back up the beach to where we left our clothes. He tugs on his jocks and t-shirt, and once I'm out of the water I do the same, sitting beside him, and reaching into the pocket of my jeans to pull out the necklace. Jasper is staring into the ocean, lost in thought, so I shift and kneel in front of him. I'm not on one knee, again not giving in to cliches.

"Jasper, baby," I start, waiting for him to look up at me. "I love you, and my world starts and ends with you. I want you by my side until the day we both leave this world."

He gasps, glancing down at the necklace in my hand. It's a simple gold chain with a heart locket.

"Are you serious?"

"Dead serious, Jasper," I reply, chuckling. "Marry me, pretty boy?"

He kisses me hard, wrapping his arms around me. "Yes, a million times yes."

He holds out his hand, and I shake my head. "I didn't get you a ring."

He gives me a cheeky pout. "Oh."

I hold up the necklace, and he leans forward. "I didn't want to do the whole cliched thing. I'll give you a ring on our wedding day."

"That sounds perfect," he replies, touching the locket with his thumb once I've clasped it around his neck.

"You're mine forever, pretty boy."

"Forever yours, Reece and Jasper until the end of time."

"Yeah, not even death will end our love," I reply, kissing him again, and pulling him into my lap. Nothing could be more perfect than having him in my arms. Jasper Capullo was always meant to be mine.

CHAPTER FORTY-FIVE

Jasper

Never would I have thought I'd be here, standing at the entrance to a church about to walk inside and down the aisle for a wedding to end the feud of my family. Even more so I didn't even entertain the thought in my head that I'd be marrying for love, and I certainly didn't think I'd also be marrying a guy who was also once my enemy.

Stepping up to the ornate wooden double doors I adjust my chocolate brown bowtie, and smooth down the fabric of my maroon suit, tracing the embroidered roses with my fingertip to calm my nerves. I'm about to marry Reece. He's going to be waiting at the end of the aisle for me, with Malyk beside him. I didn't want my father to give me away to Reece. That stupid tradition seems archaic to me. I've already given my heart to Reece, and my father had given his blessing before Reece proposed. There is only one person I want by my side and she's running late–crashing through the outside doors just as Moonlight Sonata starts to play–still tugging on her high heels as she stumbles towards me. I sigh with relief.

"Oh thank heavens you're here, Nanc. I thought I was going to have to walk down the aisle by myself."

She laughs softly. "You honestly think I'd let you do that?"

I shake my head. "No, but you had me worried for a minute."

"Sorry, I couldn't get this blasted dress done up," she replies, smoothing down the front of the strapless beige dress that hugs her body.

"Well, it looks great on you."

"You look amazing in this suit. Reece won't know what's hit him."

"Thanks," I reply, listening out for the change in the music that's my cue.

"Ready to get married?" Nancy asks, linking her arm with mine.

"More than ready," I respond, stepping through the doors and slowly walking down the aisle. The music is solemn but it's our vibe. It brings memories of that morning when Reece bent me over the piano to mind, and I smirk, willing my dick to stay down and not cause a scene.

As I walk down the long aisle I glance at our guests, friends and families. We'd requested all our guests wear Venetian masks, so there is no sides. Our wedding is a coming together of feuding families, an end to tyranny of the past. It takes my breath away, but my heart skips a beat when the final notes of Moonlight Sonata end and I'm stepping up to the altar. Reece looks gorgeous, devastatingly handsome in a black suit–and shirt– with gold embroidered details on the lapels and collar. It causes his ocean blue eyes to sparkle. Nancy turns to me and kisses my cheek, whispering, "Love you, Jasp."

I kiss her cheek in return, and smile as she steps aside and Reece steps forward to take my hand.

We face the Pastor, and he nods to ask if we're ready to begin. We affirm with a nod in return, Reece squeezing my hand in his and smiling at me way to wickedly for being a church. The pastor then begins the ceremony with the words, "People of Vemore, we're here today to celebrate the ending of the feud, through the love Reece and Jasper, as they promise each other their continued love and commitment in marriage. And the joining of their families.

"Before we get started, take a minute to look at the person sitting next to you. Whether you're of

Monserrat or Capullo descent each of you are a special part in their story, and are part of a community they're incredibly happy to be a part of. You make them feel accepted, appreciated, and loved, just the way they are. Please keep being open minded and hold love in your hearts as we get these two married!"

"Hell yeah!" Reece bellows, laughing when the Pastor scowls at him for saying hell in church and interrupting.

"Sorry Pastor," I respond.

"Forgiven Jasper. May we continue?"

"Yes, please do."

He nods again, and continues, "Not too long ago, this wedding would have been impossible, with these two being enemies, their love forbidden. But now they're elated that you're here to celebrate with them today, to witness the love they share. It is a truth that genuine love is not something that can be taught by another. Love comes from deep within the soul, an intrinsic part of what makes us human. It's a passionate means of self expression that can—and has in this case—overcome the greatest of obstacles."

I sniff back the tears in my eyes. I had no idea the Pastor was going to say such heartfelt words about love, about our relationship and how it's brought our families together. Reece squeezes my hand again. It's comforting. The pastor then continues, "Reece and Jasper's relationship shows beyond doubt that passion, and love that overcomes all." I appreciate his words but I'm anxious to get the ceremony over, worried that once again—like when I woke up with Reece at my bedside—that I'm dreaming. But when the Pastor speaks again I know it's no dream, "Marriage is a step in life, a commitment to love and take care of each other. Are you ready to take this step together?"

"Yeah!" Reece and I both chorus together, causing the pastor to let out a soft chuckle, our guests doing the same.

"Do you promise to show care towards each other, to give compassion and grace, and to always lean towards love and the understanding of one another?"

We'd practiced this part so respond, "Yes, we do."

"And do you promise to honour each other, each and every day as partners, friends, and lovers, in sickness and in health, in good times and bad, for as long as you both shall live?"

Again we loudly respond, "Yes, we do!"

The pastor again softly chuckles. "I thought that might be so! Now, you've chosen to exchange rings as a physical symbol of your vow to each other. May we have the rings?"

Malyk steps forward, reaching into the pocket of his extravagant white and purple suit. The gold bands he pulls out and hands to the pastor are engraved with R 🖤 J on the outside–for mine–and J 🖤 R for Reece's, with 'I love thee, forever' inside of both. I'm feeling giddy. This is it, the culmination of the ceremony with Reece and me making a commitment to each other for all to see. He hands Reece the ring for me, and Reece holds it in his fingers as he turns to face me.

"As you place this ring on Jasper's finger please affirm your vows to him," the pastor requests.

Reece holds my left hand, sliding the ring on my finger as he looks at me, and exhales before speaking, "Jasper, I give you this ring as a symbol of my love and devotion. I didn't choose to love you, it just hit me from the moment I saw you across the room at the frat ball that you were the one. I had no idea who you were, but that didn't matter. You are meant to be mine, and I'll love you from this moment on until my dying breath and beyond."

I stare into his eyes, sniffing back the tears cascading down my cheeks. His words–his undeniable love–make me so happy.

The pastor hands me Reece's ring, repeating the words from earlier, "As you place this ring on Reece's finger please affirm your vows to him."

"Reece, I give you this ring as a symbol of my love and devotion. I'm sorry for resisting you, and pushing you away when from the moment I met you I knew my heart belonged to you. You're everything I ever hoped for in a partner, and as I am yours, you are mine. I'll love you in this life and the next."

I slip the ring onto his finger, and he smiles so wide I swear his face is going to break. The pastor smiles at us both as we take each other's hands again, turning back to face him.

"Thank you both for those beautiful heartfelt declarations of your love. Now as you go forward in life together, remember to always have each other's best interests at heart, as well as the love and support of your families and the Vemore community."

Reece and I nod, and I squeeze his hand in mine causing him to turn his gaze to mine and give me a cheeky wink.

"With this in mind, it's my honour and right as a member of this community to pronounce you husband and husband – married! You may kiss!"

"Oh hell yeah!" Reece roars, turning towards me fully and grabbing me around the waist, dipping me low as he crashes his lips to mine in a hard, passionate kiss that causes my heart to race and our guests to holler and clap around us.

Breaking the kiss, and bringing me upright, Reece whispers, "Can't wait for tonight, husband."

My cheeks heat with a blush as we turn to face our guests raising our joined hands, and Reece hollers at the top of his lungs, "He's my husband!"

Our guests cheer, and Reece and I walk down the aisle together with our guests following beyond us as we exit the church as husbands, two guys who fell in love and united our feuding families. From enemies, forbidden to associate to lovers, and partners in life until forever.

EPILOGUE

REECE

A Year Later

The past year since Jasper and me got married has been a whirlwind. He'd quit his art history degree, we'd moved into a house together overlooking Middle Beach, between the sides of Vemore. Our love had united the city, but there was still two territories and some community members still hadn't let go of the past, despite all that had happened. One of those being Tidus. He still has it in for me, even though I've shown him that I'm not going to break his cousins' heart. He needs to lighten up, and get the pole out of his arse, or have a dick shoved up there. He denies he's gay, but I've seen the way he looks at Malyk. And my best friend is tight lipped. If they're hooking up he's not kissing–fucking–and telling. Kinda pisses me off, but I don't let my anger get to me anymore. I let it out by fucking my husband rough.

It's not like Jasper doesn't love every second of it when I fuck him rough. He's always been a brat, that certainly hasn't changed by putting a ring on his finger. That's not all that's changed in our lives. All the changes have been full on, but the most amazing one–other than our feud ending wedding–is what's happening now. Jasper's art is in the Vemore gallery and it's opening night. I'm so damn proud of him. His paintings are stunning, epic landscapes mostly except for his showcase piece of me, with every one of my tattoos intricately painted as though it's a photo. My husband is insanely talented. I'm staring at the painting of myself, thinking back to when he painted it–in his art studio in our house–and we ended up fucking and getting paint everywhere, when I feel arms wrap around my waist.

And his soft chuckle in my ear. "How're you not full of yourself, baby?"

I turn to kiss him. "I'm just admiring my sexy husband's painting. I don't see that it's me, but that you painted it. I see you through my eyes."

"That's sweet, Ree. I love you."

"I love you more Jasp, and I'm so proud of you."

He steps back, and takes my hand. "Thanks. I'm so happy to be living this dream, with you by my side."

"Always, and forever, Jasper Capullo-Montserrat."

"Always, and forever and beyond, Reece Capullo-Montserrat." He gives me another kiss, and we turn our attention to the stage where my flamboyant best friend is sashaying onto the stage in booty shorts, and a sparkly magenta bandeau top with peacock feathers sprawling from his back. Jasper gives me a wink.

"You organise this?"

"Yeah, Malyk wanted to perform. To show that art comes in many forms."

"Nice," I respond watching as Malyk dances all over the stage to the electronica, rave remix of Titanium. He's like a blur of colour on the stage, mesmerising the entire crowd of people gathered in the room. No one can tear their eyes from him.

Once the song ends, he slides a microphone onto the front of the stage. And his eyes find mine and Jasper's across the room.

"Hey fuckers, thanks for coming along tonight to celebrate Jasper's sick artwork. It's a pleasure to see you all here, and it's one hundred percent a celebration as Jasper has just purchased this art gallery!"

Malyk starts clapping—and everyone else joins in—and I turn to Jasper shocked.

"Is he serious?"

"Yep, I wanted to wait until tonight to tell you."

The applause dies down and I kiss him hard and passionately. "I'm so proud of you, Jasper. I love you more than words could ever say."

He doesn't respond, just takes my hand in his tighter and leads me through the crowd to the very back of the art gallery that's now his. He kisses me deeper, pushing me against the wall possessively.

This is where I'm supposed to be. I'm home. And all my Malicious Desires towards Jasper have been tamed. He's my everything, until my dying breath.

THE END

MALICIOUS DESIRES

ACKNOWLEDGEMENTS

Hello once again lovely readers!
Thank you so much for reading another book of
mine. I truly love sharing my words with you all.
This book has been completely different for me
to write, my first dive into a dark romance and I
loved every minute of it.
It was a book of healing for me after leaving my
husband (now ex husband-bring on divorce) of ten
years.
And I appreciate all the support of people who
have been eager to read this book from the
moment I started teasing it. I'm not going to single
people out this time but I love you all and
appreciate each and every one of you!
If you've enjoyed this story, then please review
on Amazon and any other platforms you can.
Signing off!

Caz May xx

MALICIOUS DESIRES

CAZ MAY